Spiral

Spiral

By

GA Howie

© 2009, 2018

Published in Australia in 2018 by;
Trenwick House Publishing.
www.trenwickhouse.com.au

ISBN 978-0-9923514-6-5 (paperback)
ISBN 978-0-9923514-7-2 (ebook)
ISBN 978-0-9923514-8-9 (mobi)

Editor; Lauren McCleary

Produced by;
Lightning Source

Cataloguing-in-Publication;

 A catalogue record for this
book is available from the
National Library of Australia

Acknowledgements:

'Get it finished. I need to know what happened.'
The above statement became something I heard whenever I showed people an excerpt from the book.

To that end, I want to acknowledge Karol and Jess. Both wanted to see how the story finished. Karol was happy to wait for the final. Jess was happy to beta-read for me.

Lauren Mc was another major player. She edited the book and helped to make it better. I look forward to many more collaborations.

I also want to send a thank you to NaNoWriMo (National Novel Writing Month, held during November every year). I started in 2012 with the beginnings to this story. Whilst I wasn't classed a 'winner' for 2012 (a winner is someone who wrote a minimum of 50,000 words over the course of the month), I did go on and finish the story. It underwent a few changes, but this is it. The final version of the manuscript.

Turn the page and enjoy the read.

Prologue

A small room,

A dimly lit room.

A figure, dark clothed and hooded,

Face obscured.

A cupboard with cushions,

Candles and bowls.

A military picture.

Kneeling,

Bowing,

Remembering,

Meditating.

Deciding.

'The date is set.'

Spoken aloud.

Candles extinguished,

Cushions replaced.

The figure rises,

A final bow.

Cupboard closed.

Figure departs.

1

1.1

The distinctly marked military truck turned the corner of the warehouse and drove along the well-lit dock to where several military personnel were waiting. The driver followed orders and reversed the truck until directed to stop. Two soldiers got out, walked to the rear, opened the door and stood waiting.

An officer approached the two soldiers.

'Lance Corporal Cullen and 2nd Lieutenant Smithson to collect the shipment, sir.'

'Papers, 2nd Lieutenant,' replied the receiving officer.

Smithson pulled a card from his pocket and handed it to the officer. The officer placed it in the reader in his hand, pressed his right thumb on the screen, waited for the beep and handed it to the lance corporal to do the same. The screen faded and turned green, the officer handed it to an aide and the officer looked up. The aide walked away and began giving orders.

'Cullen, Smithson.' The officer nodded once. 'It won't take long to load. Do you have an escort?'

'No, sir. Our C.O. thought it'd be quiet enough,' replied Cullen.

'Very well. It's a dark enough night.'

'The trip should be quick, considering the cargo.'

The three men stepped to one side as a trolley was wheeled to the back of the truck and four soldiers began to load the barrels of D6.

Jacobus looked on in wonder.

'What's so exciting, kid?'

'I've never been around this much explosive before.'

'Then I hope you drive better going back than getting here,' said Damian, smiling.

'Was the road rough coming down?' asked the officer.

'No, it wasn't,' replied Jacob. 'With respect, Sir, I'm the best damned driver on the base!'

'Yes, he is,' said Damian.

'Not even you've beaten me, Sir,' said Jacob.

Damian laughed.

The aide appeared at the officer's side and handed him the reader.

'Looks like we're done here. I just need your thumb once more, Damian, and you can depart.'

He obliged and climbed into the truck, where Jacob was waiting to drive the shipment back to base.

Once they'd left the warehouse precinct, Jacob drove cautiously through the back streets of Williamstown.

'You don't have to be that much of a namby-pamby driver,' said Damian, smiling.

'Shut it, Sir. I've never driven 750kgs of D6 before. Who wants this much explosive anyway?'

'It's the annual supply order and we've drawn the short straws for pickup.'

'Great, thanks.'

They left Williamstown and continued along the back roads to their home base in Laverton. They turned a corner on the edge of an industrial estate to see a broken-down vehicle blocking their way. As they got closer, they could see the bonnet up and in the vehicle's dim lights, they could see steam.

'What do you reckon, Jacob?' said Damian.

'Our orders are not to stop but bring the supply immediately back to base.'

'Indeed they are. However ...'

'However, they are blocking our way, so we should either render help,' said Jacob, 'Or turn around and find another way around. If the stranger is in trouble, we should at least see what's happening. It is one in the morning, after all.'

'Agreed.'

'What if it's an emergency?'

'I agree, we can't leave them, but we can't delay either,' said Damian. 'Do you have a suggestion?'

'We can stop; see what's the matter; call back to the base for assistance and keep going. Maximum stop, five minutes.'

'I can handle that.'

'I'll keep the truck running, and I'll keep you covered,' said Jacob. 'You go and see what's happening.'

'You're the junior, you're going to see what's happening. I'll jump into the driver's seat.'

Jacob nodded, parked the truck about ten metres from the broken-down vehicle, and activated hi-beam to illuminate the scene. He climbed down, gun at the ready. 'Is everything all right here?'

There was no reply.

Jacob moved closer and approached along the far side of the vehicle. As he moved into the shadow of the raised hood, this blocked him from Damian's sight. Jacob saw a figure in black bending over the steaming engine.

'Is everything alright?' asked Jacob as he came around to the front of the car, his gun at the ready.

The figure stood and fired a single, silenced shot at Jacob.

Damian heard the pop and raced from the cabin of the truck. Nervous, he approached the front of the stricken vehicle along the side facing the truck.

'Hey, Jacob, you okay?'

There was no response.

He stepped around to front and saw Jacob's legs on the ground. Rushing to his side, he knelt beside his dead body.

'Shit.'

Damian then froze as he felt cold steel pressing against the back of his neck.

'Drop the rifle.'

Damian moved slowly. With the handgun now at his temple, he was directed to the rear of the truck.

'Open it!'

Damian fumbled.

'Now!'

Damian swiped his card, and then pressed his shaking thumb to the lock. It glowed red and didn't open.

'Calm down and try again!'

Damian looked at the person behind him, turned back, controlled his breathing and swiped the card again. This time his hand was steadier and after pressing his thumb to the pad, the lock clicked open. Damian removed the lock and opened the doors.

'Climb in.'

Damian climbed in, the figure closely behind. Damian was forced to open one of the drums and remove one of the five-kilogram bags of D6. After the drum was re-sealed, the figure climbed down. He had Damian pass him the bag, which was placed on the ground. Damian was ordered to get out and as he did, he faked a fall and tried to tackle the figure. Moving quicker than anticipated, Damian found himself at the end of several kicks to various parts of his body and was sprawled on the ground panting and in pain.

Damian was forced to his feet clutching his ribs. In pain, he was made to reseal the truck. He was then told to get back into the cabin. He sat and turned to face his attacker.

'Give me the keys!'

Damian leant forward slightly, removed the keys and handed them over. As he looked up, he was shot between the eyes. The bullet passed through his brain, spreading a good deal of it onto the driver's seat and the window behind it.

Damian's body was dragged from the truck and placed in the back of the dark vehicle. His weapons and comms were removed before being wrapped in a heavy black plastic sheet. Next, the equally dead and disarmed body of Cullen was loaded into the back of the vehicle. The bullet used to dispatch Damian was located and removed from the back of the military truck's cabin. The keys were placed in Damian's pocket. The hood of the "stranded" vehicle was closed, and it silently and darkly drove away.

Thirty minutes later, as the first hint of a sunrise glowed on the horizon, the vehicle approached the rear of a warehouse and was driven down a ramp to a sub-basement. The figure placed a mask over its face, then the plastic bags containing the bodies of the dead soldiers were placed into two separate drums. Into each drum a green liquid was poured. As the plastic was exposed to the liquid, an acrid smoke began to drift into the sub-basement. A switch was activated on one wall, which started up the exhaust fans. The D6 was secured in a locker on another wall.

As the drums sat stewing in their liquid, heavy trucks began their daily, and very noisy, work schedule at the concrete plant opposite the warehouse. The drums were hauled across the warehouse and placed next to a press. The drums were inspected and when passed as satisfactory, a heavy disk was fitted neatly into the top. The first drum was placed on the press' base plate and the controls activated. The heavy plate was lowered and crushed its contents. The contents of the second drum were similarly crushed. When complete, the drums were sealed and loaded onto the back of a small, matte-black utility and covered with a tarpaulin. The mask was removed and thrown into a nearby bin.

A door in the far left corner opened and closed.

1.2

Corporal Jake North parked his car, smoothed over his new uniform and placed the cap on his head. He greeted other officers as he walked up the steps of the year-old offices of the Defence Force Investigative Service (DFIS). He stopped for a moment, let the others past, smiled and walked inside.

He was directed to level four where he found his desk; neat, clean and sparse. It was just on 0800 when the announcement was made for all staff to meet in the lecture theatre on level 1.

Jake walked into the room with one hundred or so others working in the DFIS office. He took a seat near the front and had his tablet ready. He turned sharply when he heard a woman's voice begin to address the room as she walked down the side aisle.

'Morning all,' she said. 'No need to stand. Most of you already know that, but the newbies won't. We're military through and through, but we're not that formal here.' She stood behind the podium, placed her tablet and pressed a few buttons. She looked over her shoulder to see the screen begin to light up. 'Very good. Welcome to everyone this morning. This will be brief as we have a lot to do. Firstly, I'd like to welcome the new recruits to DFIS. Yes, yes, stand up.'

Jake stood nervously and acknowledged those around him.

'For you newbies, I'm LCmdr. Linda Barrow. Most call me Linda, but when the occasion arises, Ma'am will suffice,' she continued. 'This is the first of the major re-assignments to happen before independence this November. In a couple of months, the various divisions of the Victorian and Tasmanian Police forces will begin to integrate.' She held up her hand as soon as she'd made her statement. 'I am fully aware that not everyone is agreeable to these wholesale changes. Never before have military and domestic police been integrated in such a way. I am a personal friend of President-elect Wordsworth and believe me when I say that we held many strong and robust discussions and arguments over this issue. In the end, I could see the value of pooling resources. It will be cost saving and it will allow us to gain valuable technology and personnel. I have already fielded many questions from you and I'm sure I will field many more. However, I want you all to know this; if I hear of any outright abuse of conduct towards any new colleague, military or police, you will have to deal with me personally. I can assure you now, you will not want that. Now for business. Every new recruit will be assigned to an existing case. You will have to learn on the run. 2ndLt Castle will assign you newbies a case. Hell, even I have to go out and get my hands dirty.' Everyone laughed. 'You oldies, be patient with the newbies. They will learn and may even be able to offer suggestions. Let's get to it.'

Linda walked away from the podium and 2ndLt David Castle stepped up.

'Your assignments are posted on the noticeboards in the incident rooms on levels three and four.'

Everyone rose to leave. Jake put his tablet in his bag and stepped into the central aisle.

'North,' said David.

Jake turned as he saw the second lieutenant approach him. 'Sir?'

'You'll be with me. We've had a report placed by Williams Defence Force Base at Laverton. It seems some of their soldiers are missing. They've located the truck they were using last night but no drivers. They reckon they've found blood on the driver's seat. Grab a camera and field kit and meet me in the garage in fifteen minutes.'

'Yes, sir,' replied Jake. He headed swiftly for his desk, grabbed his new digital camera, found out where kits could be collected from and rushed into the garage.

'North, over here.' Jake turned and saw David at a window. He turned and walked away with a set of keys in his hand. 'Stow your gear and climb in. I'll drive.'

They headed out of the underground garage and turned onto the main road.

'There should be a copy of the preliminary report on your tablet. Have a look at it and give me your thoughts,' said David, glancing over to Jake.

Jake accessed the file and began to read;

Date: Wednesday, January 8

Time: 0730

Location: Laverton

Details: 2ndLt. Damian Smithson and L. Cpl Jacobus Cullen were on a return trip to the Williamstown delivery centre with a shipment of 750kgs of D6. Due to arrive back at base at around 0500, they still had not returned by 0600. An extensive search was conducted and at approximately 0700, the empty truck was located. Neither soldier was with the truck and blood was noticed on the back of the driver's seat. The rear of the truck appears to be unopened. DFIS have been notified.

'That's pretty short,' said Jake, putting his tablet back in his bag. 'Also, they're MPs from Williams, not regular soldiers. I worked with them both. Without sounding dramatic, this is almost personal.'

'No need to waffle on,' replied David. 'How well did you know them?'

'I was at Williams for only a couple of years, but it was a roller coaster. I actually got on well enough with Smithson and Cullen.'

'One step at a time, kid. Also, you'll have to learn to keep emotions out of these events. For the most part it's good but when it comes to someone you know, it's a lot harder. Do you want me to take you back to base?'

'No sir, I will be able to do what we came to do,' said Jake. 'How long before we arrive?'

'According to the NAV, it should be another fifteen minutes.'

'What do you want me to do when we get there?' asked Jake.

'Start by photographing everything, especially the alleged blood. Look for any anomalies with the truck. I'll start dusting.'

Jake nodded.

You're quiet?' asked David, after ten minutes of silent travel. 'Everything okay?'

'It's fine, Sir. Thinking about the missing men.'

'You can call me David. We're a little less formal in DFIS. It makes for a better and more productive environment. So, what's up?'

'I wasn't expecting to be in the field quite so quickly,' said Jake.

'Understandable. It's usually a few days, or even weeks, of case assimilation before that happens. However, in your case, I thought it best.'

'In my case?' Jake asked guardedly.

'Nothing's wrong. Quite the opposite,' responded David. 'Your application was very impressive and even though you're not supposed to know this, you scored the highest entry mark since the inception of DFIS.'

Jake blushed and looked out the window. David laughed.

'I want to see if you're as good as you say you are.'

Jake turned sharply, slightly surprised. 'I'll do my best.'

'I'd expect nothing less.'

They turned a corner and spied the truck ahead. A lone MP guarding it. David pulled their car to a halt and they got out. Jake retrieved the camera and kit from the back and walked up beside David.

'Well, well, well,' said the guard. 'If it isn't the goody-two shoes L.Cpl. Jake North. Fancy meeting you here.'

Jake looked and smiled wryly. 'That's Crpl Jake North, thanks.'

The guard snapped to attention and saluted.

Jake returned the salute. 'You can relax, Harrison,' said Jake and then he turned to David. 'LtCpl. Will Harrison and I used to work together in the MPs at Williams before I transferred.'

Great, Jake thought. *Here I was thinking I'd moved on from having to deal with Harrison.*

'Then why the remark about your rank then?' asked David.

Jake shifted nervously. 'For as long I was at Williams, my rank was always lower. I only ranked equal to him just before I left, but that didn't stop him using length of service to cause me grief.'

David stepped in front of Harrison, who was still standing at attention. Harrison looked steadfastly forward.

'LtCpl?'

'Yes, sir?'

'Is this true?'

Harrison remained quiet.

'Very well, I understand,' said David.

David stepped away and to the side.

'At ease soldier,' responded David. 'What can you tell me, Harrison?'

'When the truck hadn't returned thirty minutes after their scheduled time, we attempted contact with no reply. When that failed, our Captain sent two of us out to look for the truck. After searching for a while, we found it here. I and another soldier inspected the vehicle. There was no sign of the two soldiers, 2ndLt. Damian Smithson and L.Cpl Jacobus Cullen. We checked the truck to find the driver's window open, the keys missing and what appears to be blood on the headrest. There was no blood on the ground and, whilst we haven't checked, the rear doors do not appear to have been opened. We filed the report with DFIS and have done nothing since.'

'Very good, Harrison,' said David. 'We'll take it from here.'

'Yes, Sir,' saluted Will and stepped back.

'Okay, Jake, get started.'

Jake nodded and began to take photographs of the truck, its proximity to the road, the driver's side door, seat, blood spatter and rear door. He walked around the truck a couple more times when he stopped alongside the front left fender. With his gloved hand, he reached over and retrieved a ten of spades playing card and a similar sized card with a raised yellow sunflower on it.

'I think it's definitely blood, David,' said Jake. 'Also, I found these.' He held up the card.

David held out a plastic bag and Jake dropped them in. 'Where were they?'

'Tucked in the corner of the bonnet by the windscreen. Not a place something like that would fall naturally. It has to have been placed.'

'We'll add that to the pile,' replied David. 'If you're done with the pics, you can take some samples. I've got some prints here, so hopefully we can see who's been handling the truck.'

Jake took samples of the blood and brain matter and the noticed the hole. He took several more photos and began to investigate. 'David, I think I've found what looks like a bullet hole, but I can't feel any bullet in there.' David came over as Jake was trying to reach behind the seat. 'I can't feel any exit point either.

'Doesn't mean there isn't one.'

'Unless the bullet has already been removed?'

'That would be unusual,' said David, thoughtfully.

David approached Will. 'Do you have authority to open the back of the truck?'

'No, Sir, I don't,' he replied. 'I can get someone here.'

'As quickly as you can please.'

Will took his radio and requested someone from the base come to the location of the truck with the means to access the cargo in the rear. At the same time, David called back to DFISHQ requesting a tow.

'Harrison,' said David, 'Get the base to send another truck. Unless the D6 has been tampered with, I don't think we'll need that for the investigation. Best we get that back to Williams as quickly as we can.'

Will nodded and radioed the request.

Once Jake had finished with the truck, he began to walk up and down the road. As he approached a spot about ten metres in front of the army truck, he spotted a small brown spot on the road. He placed a small ruler beside it and took a photograph. 'David, you wanna come and have a look at this? Can you bring the kit too, please?'

David came over and looked at the brown spot.

'Blood?' asked Jake.

'We'll soon find out,' said David. He took a cotton swab and rubbed it over the brown spot. Then he dripped a few drops of liquid onto the cotton tip. Almost instantly, it changed colour.

Showing it to Jake, he smiled and bagged the sample.

'Has to be the second soldier,' said Jake. 'There's no way a single spot of blood could get from that cabin to here.'

'We'll wait and see but I agree. Have you seen any more samples?'

'Not yet,' said Jake.

'Harrison,' called David. Will came to where they were. 'Has anyone been around this area this morning?'

'Not that I can recall.'

'Where did your vehicle park when they found the truck?'

'Behind it. Then when we left, we took a wide berth so probably would've missed this spot.'

'Thanks, Harrison,' said David.

Thirty minutes later, with Jake and David waiting by their SUV, the DFIS tow truck arrived followed by Jeepney. Ten minutes after that, an identical army truck to the abandoned one also arrived. Several officers alighted from all the newly arrived vehicles. Those from DFIS went and spoke with David and Jake. Those from the defence force spoke with Harrison.

'Here they come, David,' said Jake, indicating with a nod the defence personnel heading in his direction.

David turned. 'Morning.' He held out his hand. The lead woman saluted his authority instead.

'Sgt Kate Wallace,' she said curtly. 'I believe you want us to unlock the truck for you?'

'Yes, I do, Sgt Wallace. I need to make sure the D6 hasn't been tampered with. Also, we need to take the truck to our HQ for further analysis. Upon initial investigation, there is no bullet resulting in the blood spatter on the seat of the cabin.'

'I expect to get this truck back as new,' said Kate.

'We'll look after it for you,' replied David. 'Once we're done, we'll put it back together and you can have it back.'

'Appreciated.' Kate walked to the back of the truck, removed a card from a pocket, swiped it and pressed her thumb when indicated. The lock went green and she removed it. 'All yours, 2ndLt.'

'Thank you.' David pulled on clean rubber gloves and opened the doors. 'Jake, can you bring the kit?'

A minute later, Jake climbed into the back with David, the snap of rubber heard once more. 'What are we looking for here?'

'Anything really. Any sign of tampering, sabotage, etc.'

'Were they carrying the detonators?'

David walked to the back of the truck. 'Sgt Wallace, was the truck carrying the detonators as well?'

'No, we dealt with those separately. They were delivered two days ago.'

'Thanks.' David returned to Jake. 'Should be safe enough. All the same, be careful.'

David and Jake began to check each of the drums.

'David, here. I think this one's been opened,' said Jake.

David had a closer look once Jake had finished taking a few photos. David ran his finger around the rim.

'Indeed it has, and it was put back and made to look sealed.' David took a scalpel from the kit and gently ran it around the rim forcing it to open sightly. He and Jake gently removed the lid.

'I dunno, looks okay to me,' said Jake.

'Sgt Wallace, could you join us in here please?' called David.

Kate climbed into the back of the truck and stood looking at the drum.

'Are you able to confirm if there's anything wrong with this drum?' asked David. 'We found that it had been opened.'

'At first glance, I couldn't tell. As to it being opened, we had confirmation electronically that when the delivery left Williamstown dock, it was fully sealed.'

'With your permission, I'd like to open another drum for comparison.'

'Granted,' said Kate.

She watched David like a hawk as he carefully opened a neighbouring drum. Removing the lid, he could see what was wrong. 'A five kilogram bag of D6 is missing from the first drum. We'll definitely need to keep this one.'

Kate breathed in deliberately, flaring her nostrils. 'How long will that be?'

'As long as it takes,' replied David, calmly. 'You can transfer the rest to the other truck. Just not this one.' David resealed the second drum and replaced the lid of the first one. 'Come on Jake, we'll let them get rid of these so we can get the truck back to HQ.'

David and Jake jumped down and removed the drum they wanted to the back of their SUV. When the rest of the drums had been removed to the other truck, the defence personnel left.

'I can only imagine in what tone my name will used at mess tonight,' smiled Jake. 'They were quite cold and Sgt Wallace didn't even acknowledge me.'

'I did notice Harrison was rather informal with you when you arrived,' said David.

'He always thought he was better than anyone else and always managed to get the cushiest of jobs.'

'Do you want to go back?' asked David, amusingly.

'I just got out of there,' replied Jake. 'They're a bit too austere for me. I discovered that when I arrived a couple of years ago.'

'Let's get this truck home.' David called for the tow truck to back up and remove the defence truck.

David and Jake followed the tow truck on its way back to DFISHQ. Once they had parked, David returned the keys.

'Check that field kit back in and get those samples to Gabby. I want to know whose blood and fingerprints these belong to. Also, go over the truck with a fine-toothed comb. I'll be working on the drum.'

'Okay.' Jake went through the kit, separated the samples and took the kit back to the quartermaster, only to find out that he had signed the kit out to himself for as long as he was with DFIS. All he needed to do was re-stock as required, which he did.

With samples in hand, and directions from the QM, he found Gabby tucked away in a corner of the first floor. There was only one entrance and it was airlocked. Jake stepped into the airlock and waited for the second door to open. As he stepped into the Lab, Jake looked around. The most interesting was the music. Loud enough to mask work noises, but not deafening. He slowly stepped further into the lab. He stopped and gently touched some of the samples that were on a shelf nearby. Lost in the moment, he was startled when the music stopped.

'Hi, Gabby?' called Jake before any music started.

'That's me, SSgt Gabby Kindregan,' she replied, bounding from behind her desk, pressing a button on a remote in her hand.

Jake was taken back for a moment. He was not expecting whom he met. Gabby Kindregan had a broad Scottish accent, bright red hair, tied back in a ponytail, and the most electric green eyes. She didn't wear a traditional lab coat, but he did see some hanging near the door.

On a table nearby sat several cans of a popular energy drink. Jake noted the brand for future reference.

'You are?' she queried. 'New?'

'Yes, yes, new. Crpl Jake North. Arrived today.'

'That's right, I saw you this morning,' she replied. 'You're quick. Samples already?'

'I was taken on an investigation right from the meeting this morning. We've only just got back.'

'Not much to check, huh?'

'Complex but not huge. Two soldiers now missing. Blood and brain matter in the cabin of the truck they were using to transport a shipment of D6. No bullet that I can find yet, and David wanted me to get these to you right away.'

'David who?' asked a man from behind Jake.

Jake swung around and flinched slightly, to see a very tall and imposing man standing there. He heard Gabby chuckle.

'Not funny,' said Jake.

'Yes it is,' said Gabby. 'Anyway, that's my boss, 2ndLt Dustin Coles. Dusty, this is Crpl Jake North.'

'Pleased to meet you Jake,' said Dustin. 'When did you start?'

'Only this morning,' he replied.

'You're quick.'

'That's what I said.'

'Trained her well, I have.'

Jake shook his head and blinked. 'Is this the lab or the funny ward?'

Dustin slapped Jake on the back. 'Welcome aboard young-one. Listen well. Learn much, you will.'

'Thank you, oh wise and wrinkled one.'

Dustin looked at him sharply. Jake froze. Dustin laughed, as did Gabby. Jake relaxed and laughed.

'One hour, be back I will. Expect results I do.' Jake bowed, smiled cheekily and left the room.

'It's nice to see a new recruit with a sense of humour,' said Dustin.

'I like him,' said Gabby.

'Oh no, not again. Be careful young lady. I do not want a repeat of last year.'

'It won't happen. He's gay.'

'How do you know that?' said Dusty, surprised. 'Did he tell you?'

'Nah, I can tell.'

'Riiight. You'd better get those samples done.'

Gabby laughed and took the samples to the bench.

Jake returned to the garage to find the truck waiting in the secure investigation bay. He grabbed his camera and kit and was directed to where he could get a tool kit. He first removed the driver's seat and examined the headrest. He found the exit hole to the seat and photographed it. Using a powerful light, he searched centimetre by centimetre over the back wall of the cabin until he found a significant dint. Noticing that the hole was deep enough to retain a bullet, he was puzzled as to its non-existence. He photographed the hole at a variety of distances. The lens even allowed him to take several macro shots of the hole. Sitting back and examining them on the screen, he noticed small metal shavings. He grabbed a sticky sample strip and removed the shavings. He then searched the rest of the truck and found nothing else unusual.

He packed up the tool kit, his field kit and camera, put the headrest on the front seat and closed the door. As he stepped into the lift, he automatically pressed the button for level four, then realised he needed to visit Gabby with the new sample. Jake stepped off at level one and made his way to the far corner where Gabby had her lab.

He entered the lab to the strains of loud classical music, but that you couldn't hear it until you passed through the airlock. He smiled as he made his way towards Gabby's back. He was stopped in his tracks when the music suddenly changed from the relaxing classical, which he didn't mind, to rather amusing and bizarre strains of a stage musical number.

At that moment, Gabby turned around.

'Ooh!' she exclaimed loudly. 'I didn't hear you come in.'

Jake opened his mouth to speak.

'Oops, sorry.' Gabby pushed the sleeve of her shirt up to reveal a remote strapped to her forearm. She tapped at the screen and the music dropped to become background ambience. 'Now, you've come for your results?'

'Yes please,' said Jake. 'You're a surprising and remarkable woman.'

'Thanks, I think.'

'It's good. All good.'

'Okay. Here you go,' she said, guiding Jake to a screen. 'Sample one, the blood from the truck's cabin, belongs to 2ndLt Damian Smithson. I doubt there'll be much of the back of his head left from the pics I saw. Nasty, and a shame. He was a nice man.'

'You've met him?'

'You could say that.' Gabby mentally reminisced for a moment.

'How do you me...' Jake smiled.

'We had a very hot four-day weekend last year, but I wanted someone more my own age.'

'I can understand that,' said Jake. 'What about the sample from the single blood spot we found?'

'That belongs to L. Cpl Jacobus Cullen.'

'Have you 'met' him too?' asked Jake.

Gabby shot him a dirty look.

'Sorry.'

'Besides, he way too ugly.'

'True, he's no model,' said Jake.

'When did you meet him?'

'My last two years were at Williams. I transferred there as a regular MP,' explained Jake. 'Being born in Victoria, I could transfer without question.'

'Ah yes, the declaration of cessation and independence from the rest of the country. I've chosen to stay, seeing as though I've made Melbourne my home now. My papers came through just before Christmas. I got in early.'

'Back to Cullen and Smithson.'

'All we know so far is who the blood belongs to. As to how or when they were killed, we'll need bodies,' replied Gabby.

'What about the playing and sunflower cards? What did you make of them?'

'Very odd. It's simple as an item, but complex in that there are absolutely no fingerprints on them at all. From what I can see online, the sunflower card is a collector card, popular in the latter half of last century. This was a common one and could've been bought from any newsagent at the time. Today, you might find them in an op shop or online, but there are no markings to indicate where it might've been purchased from. As for the playing card, it's very common. There's no way we can trace where it may have been purchased. Although there is a hole in it.' Gabby held up the card to shoe Jake where the hole was.

'Something to begin with. Also, I found these in an indentation behind the headrest. I thought the bullet hadn't penetrated the headrest because I couldn't feel anything. I've since found out it did go through and was probably lodged in the back of the cabin, but all I could find were these metal shavings. Can you do anything with these?' said Jake.

'It'll be hard without some form of reference, but I'll see what they're made of and let you know.'

'Great, thanks. Also, I'll send you the pics of the hole, if that'll help.'

'Either they will or they won't,' said Gabby.

'I'll go back to my desk and have them for you soon.'

'Thanks, young-one.'

Jake smiled and left the lab. He was still smiling when he got back to his desk.

'What are you so happy about?' asked David, as he watched Jake sit down.

'Nothing really,' he replied.

'What have you found in the truck?'

Jake connected the camera to his computer and began to download the latest pics. 'This is all that's of interest in the cabin. The bullet went right through and hit the rear wall, but there's no bullet. I found some metal shavings in the in-dentation.' Jake pointed to them on the screen. 'I dropped them off in the lab.'

'Very good. What about the blood?'

'I got those results as well. The blood in the cabin was that of Smithson and the single spot on the ground matches Cullen. All we need now are the bodies.'

'We have no clues there, yet,' said David.

'What about prints? Gunshot residue?' asked Jake.

'Well, the only fingerprints I could find were those of Cullen and Smithson. Nothing else. If the soldiers have been killed, then whoever did this knew what they were doing and knew not leave any evidence behind.'

'Someone trained then?'

'You think so, North?'

'If it were a regular robbery, we'd have a bullet, bodies, damage to the lock ... I just thought of something.' Jake rose suddenly and left the office, grabbing his tablet on the way.

Curious, David followed him.

'What's the matter?' asked Jake.

'I'm curious to see where you're off to in such a hurry,' replied David.

They rode the lift to the basement garage and Jake strode to the rear of the truck. He removed the lock from the floor of the back of the truck, placed it in an evidence bag and headed back to the lift. Getting off at level 1, Jake crossed the floor to the lab.

'You still here, Gabby?' Jake called.

'Sure am, sweetie. What's up?'

Jake walked up to where Gabby was working and placed the lock on the bench.

'Are you able to determine who's accessed this lock?'

Gabby picked up the bag with the lock and turned it around. 'I should be able to. Has this been processed?'

'Yep. I only brought it in the bag to preserve any prints

or other info.'

'Good thinking, Junior.'

Jake laughed.

'Let's see.' Gabby removed the lock with gloved hands and inspected it more closely. 'I have a cable that can connect that to the computer.' She walked to a cupboard and rummaged around in a large blue plastic tub. She emerged holding a length of black cable with mini-usb jacks on each end. Jake watched as she plugged one end into the lock and the other into a bank of outlets near a screen.

'Watch the screen. See Gabby do her magic.' The screen filled with dozens of rows of data. 'Looks like these are in date order.' She scrolled back to the top and went to the top of the list. 'This is the last entry. All we have to do is verify whose access code this is and we'll know when it was accessed.'

Jake pulled his tablet from its pouch over his shoulder and tapped away. 'Here it is, that code belongs to 2ndLt Damian Smithson. What time was it accessed?'

'Right there,' said Gabby, pointing to the screen.

'Great, that gives us a time.'

'Jake, there was an attempt seconds before the last one. Same codes. It looks like this lock uses a swipe card and thumb print recognition.'

'Who else used it that night?'

Gabby and Jake went over the first several records.

'There's only a few really, as the date changes,' said Jake.

'Whose is the other code here?' asked Gabby.

'Let me check.' Jake referred to his tablet. 'That belongs to LtCpl Jacobus Cullen. So, Smithson had an unsuccessful attempt immediately followed by a successful one. That would be when the D6 was stolen. An hour earlier, Cullen and Smithson used the lock seconds apart.'

'Most likely to seal the lock after the shipment had been placed inside,' interrupted David, as he entered the lab.

'Hmmm. Prior to that Cullen and Smithson access it twice.'

'Again, I'd say that would when they unlocked it at Williamstown dock and before that to seal the back of the truck before they left Williams base,' added David.

'Thanks, Gabby, you're a gem.' Jake leant over and kissed her on the cheek. Grabbing his tablet, he left the lab, David following.

Jake turned to wave to see a stunned Gabby at the desk.

David leant in one corner of the lift and smiled at Jake.

'What's that smirk for?' asked Jake.

'I was told you were good, but you're doing better than I expected so quickly.'

Jake looked at the ground. 'Thanks.'

'What made you have the lock checked?' asked David, as they got out on their level.

'As I was going over the checklist of what might've happened, it suddenly hit me that with a regular robbery, that lock would most likely have been destroyed. So I wanted to see who accessed it as that is the only way anyone could've gained entry to the rear of the truck.'

'Very good. It probably would've taken me another day to work that one out. What do you think now?'

'I usually like to go home and mull over the information I have first,' said Jake, sitting at his terminal and adding the latest information to the file. 'In the meantime, I think we are possibly dealing with someone who knows the system and knew how to get access to the truck. They knew that evidence would be gathered and so removed the bullet.'

'Why didn't they clean the blood away then?'

'They wanted us to know that we won't be finding those soldiers alive.'

'Smithson at least,' said David.

'I doubt Cullen will be alive either. They wouldn't leave one alive and one dead.'

'True.'

'Where to next?' asked Jake.

'Home for tonight,' replied David. 'We'll take it up again tomorrow.'

'Yes, Sir.'

David went to his desk, whilst Jake finalised his notes. He downloaded a copy of the file to his tablet, switched everything off and gathered his stuff and went home.

1.3

Jake walked into his recently purchased house in Yarraville. Boxes filled rooms along with materials gathered for the renovations he was going to do. He dropped his satchel onto the bed, had a shower and changed into loose fitting pants and a top.

Plugging his smart phone into the dock on the stereo in the lounge room, he chose the program he wanted. Unrolling a mat he kept in the corner, he began to go through a series of stretches and exercises. When complete, he sat on the mat, crossed his legs, placed his palms on his thighs and closed his eyes.

- Army truck late,

- Then found abandoned.

- Soldiers missing, probably dead.

- Blood on the seat.

- No bullet.

- Lock not tampered with.

- Unsuccessful unlock attempt.

- Successful unlock.

- Possibly forced unlock unsuccessful,

- Possibly forced unlock successful,

- D6 missing.

- No bodies.

- Blood samples confirm soldiers rostered for delivery.

- Back streets used.

- Possible known route back to base.

- Investigate if travel plans logged.

- Perp knew details.

- Investigate illegal computer access.

- Perp intimate with protocols.

- Possibly ex-military.

- Re-check crime scene for surveillance.

- Check satellites.

Jake sat for several more minutes as he meditated and quietened his mind. When he finished, he slowly rose, stretched and retrieved his tablet from his bedroom. Sitting on the edge of the bed, he made a few notes from his thoughts for the following day.

2.1

The dark figure moved quietly through the unlocked front gate of the building site. The security guard had just left in his car. The figure hid in the shadows of the office and watched as he saw the two men move about on the dimly lit second level. The dark figure moved further along until he came to the storage locker. Quietly opening the door, the figure crept inside. After searching for a few moments, the figure found what it was looking for. Placing several of the items into the back pack, the figure crept back towards the door.

Through the still night, he clearly heard two men talking.

'Jack, will you make sure the locker is closed? I haven't checked it yet.'

'Will do, Vic. I'll go and do it now.'

The dark figure quickly and quietly slipped out of the locker and ducked around the corner, but not before Jack caught a glimpse.

'Hey, you, stop. What are you doing?' called Jack and hurried to where he saw the dark figure turn the corner.

As the man turned the corner he was grabbed around the neck. He cried out, but his head was snapped sharply to one side and he fell limply to the ground.

Vic Forde was an average looking man. He's 183 cm tall, solid and walked with a cane. Vic worked for a construction company, who were building a new residential and commercial complex in the west of Melbourne. He was overseeing the last of the night crew, working a half shift to correct some problems caused by a third-party company not following plans exactly. His phone began to vibrate in his pocket and he reached down and grabbed it. The caller ID revealed it was his partner. 'What's up, Dawn?' he said.

He heard heavy breathing from the other end.

'Baby...' more heavy breathing. 'Now...'

'Okay. I'm leaving work. I'll meet you at the hospital as soon as I can. I love you.' All Vic heard as he hung up was another moan.

He quickly walked to the edge of the second level he was checking. He turned suddenly at a sound he thought he heard, but there was nothing or no one there. Being the end of the shift, only he and Jack, his assistant for the night, remained. A muffled cry made him rush to the railing.

In the glow of the arc lights, he saw Jack below wearing a hard hat and hobbling around holding his shin.

'I'll only be another five minutes or so, Jack. You okay?'

The figure below waved. Damian went back to the centre of the floor and checked various pieces of machinery, which took him closer to ten minutes. Damian turned suddenly at the sound of metal on metal. Something fell past the edge of the open floor. Damian moved to the barrier and peered over the edge.

A pair of legs gripped Vic firmly around the neck. He let out a brief gasp of surprise. His head was rapidly snapped to left, breaking his neck, and he dropped instantly to the floor, dead. The body was pushed over the edge, falling to the ground below. This was followed soon after by the cane.

Even with the dust still settling around the body, it was wrapped in black plastic. A large four-wheel utility was reversed to where the body lay. The wrapped body of Vic Forde was loaded into the back of the utility parked inside the yard. A second plastic wrapped body was placed beside Vic's.

After a few final arrangements at the site, the construction utility was driven to a warehouse, about ten minutes away. As the ute approached the rear of the complex, the door was activated remotely. The construction ute was driven to the sub-basement and parked beside a matte-black truck already housed there.

Grabbing a fresh mask, two more drums were rolled from where they had been stored in one corner. The first was loaded onto a trolley then placed at the rear of the construction ute. One of the bodies was dragged from the tray and roughly shoved into the drum. This was then wheeled and placed beside a large press. This was repeated for the second body.

Once both drums were standing beside the press, green liquid was poured in until the bodies were covered. These were then left alone. The construction ute was thoroughly cleaned and wiped down. At the completion of this task, it was driven out of the warehouse and returned to the building site. It was reversed up to the front gate. The gate was checked and made to look like the task of locking up hadn't been finished. The cabin was then quickly wiped down and left for the morning shift to find.

The dark figure returned to the warehouse where the recently handled drums were inspected. A heavy plate was positioned in the top of each. In the early morning light, with the sound of heavy machinery drifting in from the concrete works opposite the warehouse, the press was activated. Pulling the lever, the heavy plate was gently pressed into the first drum, crushing the contents into the liquid. Some of the purged liquid was caught in the tray under the press. The drum was placed to one side as the second drum was pressed.

When complete, the drums were sealed and placed on the back of the black truck, next to the other two drums. Minutes later, a door in the far left corner opened and closed.

2.2

Dan Markeet arrived at the work site to find Vic Forde's truck reverse parked against the main gate. That was unusual thing number one. Unusual thing number two was that there were no keys in it. Unusual thing number three was the locked gate itself. There was the padlock and the chain but they were not in the correct position.

Dan took his keys from his pocket and opened the gate carefully. He absent-mindedly breathed a sigh of relief. He stopped for a moment, suddenly uneasy. He crossed the yard slowly in the direction of the main huts. At the far end was the primary storage locker. He checked the lock without touching it to find it secure. He went into the main office and checked the log. Dan confirmed that Vic had indeed logged in for the night shift but had not logged out, nor had one of the other workers. Everyone else had logged out correctly. He also couldn't find the paperwork for the night shift. His puzzlement was now turning to concern. As he walked towards the entrance to the building, he saw the scuff and drags marks in the dirt. At that point he stopped, returned to the office and called the police.

Dan waited at the main gate. As other workers arrived, he stopped them from entering due to the odd circumstances and the fact that he'd called the police. He also tried calling Vic, but it kept going to voicemail. Dan checked the roster to see that Vic wasn't due until at least lunchtime anyway. He was still concerned and kept that to himself, but at the same time was growing frustrated with his workers who were insisting they be allowed to get to work.

Just as Dan was about to explode, the first police car arrived. This shut his workers up instantly. However, they began to crowd in to hear what was going on.

The female police officer approached first. 'Who made the call about the missing workers?' she asked.

'I did,' replied Dan.

'Snr.Const. Aimee McManus. Normally we don't respond until they've been missing for at least twenty-four hours, but as you were insistent, we agreed to come down.'

'Thank you, Snr.Const. Normally I would've done the same, but Vic wouldn't leave his truck parked this way and not leave his keys,' explained Dan. 'Also, I'd like you to take a look at scuff marks on the ground.'

Aimee turned to another officer who was approaching them. 'Constable, stay here and don't let anyone in,' said Aimee.

'Yes, Ma'am.'

'Lead on, Mr...?'

'Oh sorry. Dan Markeet, project manager for this site.'

'Lead on Mr. Markeet.'

Dan led the Snr.Const to the spot he saw the scuff marks on the ground. She studied them carefully. She let Dan explain what he thought and she agreed with most of his summations. Aimee then listened as Dan explained how he found the lock on the gate, the position of the unmoved truck and the lock on the storage locker. Dan also explained that Vic or the other worker had not clocked off last night, nor had Vic finished any of the paperwork, which wasn't like him at all.

'I'll call in the detectives and see what they think,' said Aimee. She walked back to her car and placed the call.

Twenty minutes later another car and two SUV's stopped outside the worksite. A suited man walked directly to Aimee.

'Aimee, good to see you,' greeted the man, yawning heavily. 'What have we got?'

'Good morning, Det.Sgt,' Aimee replied. 'Are you just finishing night shift?'

'No, I was at the hospital with Dawn,' he said.

'Why were you at the hospital?'

'Dawn rang me when Vic didn't show up.'

'How is she?'

'Not good. She lost the baby last night.'

'Damn. Is she okay?'

'She'll be in hospital a while, but she'll be okay. She's a tough woman.'

'Don't I know it,' said Aimee.

'Once I'm done here, I'm heading back there.'

'You shouldn't have come at all, Brad.'

'It'll keep my mind off things,' said Brad. 'What's going on?'

Aimee relayed the story of the missing men, the slightly askew gate lock, the missing paperwork and showed him the scuff marks on the ground. When Aimee had finished, she introduced Brad to Dan.

'Dan Markeet, this is Det.Sgt Brad Mallinson,' said Aimee.

They shook hands.

'Morning, Dan,' said Brad. 'Snr.Const McManus tells me that one of the men missing is a Vic Forde? Is this correct?'

'Yes, it is Det.Sgt,' replied Dan. 'Is he in trouble with the police?'

'Not exactly, but sort of.'

'I don't understand.'

'Did you know that Forde's partner was Det.Snr.Sgt Dawn Forde?'

'No, I didn't. I knew his partner's name was Dawn, but he never really talked about what she did, even if she did work. Are you sure we have the same man?'

'We can talk about that later,' said Brad. 'I want forensics in here looking for clues. If we have the same man, he should've been at the hospital last night. The fact that he didn't turn up at all is not good. Coupled with what may have happened here, I want to make sure. You might as well let your men go for the day, they won't be doing anything here.'

'I'll need to have the shift supervisor and our safety manager on site. Insurance won't let us have anyone on site otherwise.'

Brad thought for a moment. 'Okay, but they will have to do what they're told.'

'I'm sure they can manage that,' said Dan. He went over, dismissed the men for the day, assuring them they would still be paid. He also made sure the shift supervisor and safety manager stayed.

'Constable, can you call for a forensics team?' said Brad

looking over at Const. Scott Glass.

'They're already here, Brad,' said Aimee. 'I called them right after I called you. Just in case.'

'You really want that promotion, huh?'

Aimee blushed.

'No harm done,' said Brad. He waved for the forensics people to come onsite. They stood in front of him. 'I want every scuff and tyre marked recorded. Dust for prints, well you know the drill. I want the report on my desk by the end of the day. If Vic has gone missing, I want to be the one to tell Dawn.'

They nodded and began working.

Dan and his men stood outside the project office and watched the police forensics team do their work. Dan happened to glance up and saw something flapping from the guardrail on the second level.

'Det.Sgt,' called Dan.

'What is it, Mr. Markeet?'

Dan explained that he'd seen something hanging off the level two guardrails at the edge. Brad looked up, saw the same thing and dispatched a forensics officer to investigate. The officer returned about ten minutes later holding up a plastic bag with a black paper parasol and a nine of diamonds playing card in it.

'Is there anything else out of place, Mr. Markeet?' asked Brad.

'Not that I can see from here,' replied Dan.

'What's that shipping container down the end used for?' asked Brad, indicating the red shipping container at the end of the row of site huts.

'That's our storage locker.'

'What's kept inside?'

'We keep general supplies, explosives, spare parts.'

'Explosives? Why do you need those on a building site?'

'When we were digging the foundations, the owners wanted more space below than was really needed. As we dug down, we came across rock that we needed to blow.'

'What did you use?'

'D6.'

'Who has access?'

'Myself, my foreman here, Vic Forde, and Jeremy Pyke.'

'Can you show me the locker?'

Dan led Brad to the locker. He showed him the security lock that required a thumbprint and five-digit numeric code.

'Do you have an inventory of the contents?'

'We check it regularly. I can get the foreman to bring it over.'

Brad nodded. Dan used his comms to ask the supervisor to get the locker inventory.

'Do you have the ability to see who accesses the lock? Both opening and closing,' asked Brad.

'We only need authority to unlock it. Anyone can lock it,' said Dan.

'Right then, don't touch it. I want it dusted before we have a look inside.' Brad got the attention of one of the forensics team, who came right over. 'I want this lock and surrounds photographed and dusted. When you're done, let me know as I need to have a look inside.' The forensics woman nodded and got to work.

Brad and Dan went back to the main office hut just as the supervisor was stepping out with a tablet in his hand.

'Once the lock has been dusted we'll take a look inside,' said Brad. 'I want to know what's missing.'

Dan and the supervisor nodded.

'Dan, you said there were two men missing,' asked Brad. 'Who's the other man?'

'Jack DeVries, one of our more experienced workers. He and Vic would've been doing the final check before securing the site for the night.'

'What time would that have been?'

'Lately, we've been having some external delivery delays and we've been doing what we can into the night. Generally, we close the site around ten, but sometimes it can be earlier.'

A knock at the door and the insertion of the forensics woman told Brad that the locker was ready to inspect. Dan, Brad and the supervisor walked along the row of huts to the locker at the end. Dan released the lock and opened the door. Dan led the way inside, followed by Brad and then the supervisor. The supervisor went to work immediately checking the contents against the inventory list.

'I see you keep the D6 itself locked separately?'

'Yes we do,' replied Dan.

'Who has access to this locker?' asked Brad.

'Only Vic and a Jeremy Pyke. He's a sub-contractor really, but occasionally we have him work shifts when we need assistance.'

'He's an explosives sub-contractor?'

'Yeah. His license checks out. We did all of that before we hired him. He's ex-military. I think he was even in the same unit as Vic.'

'Where did they serve?'

'I think I heard them talking about it one day and it sounded like it was about ten years ago, but I didn't hear where they were stationed.'

'Thanks. Can you get this Jeremy Pyke to come down? I'd like to know that everything is okay in there.'

Dan and Brad stepped outside and Dan rang Jeremy. After insisting it was his day off, Jeremy said he'd be there as soon as he could.

Jeremy arrived an hour later. He was puzzled as to the police constable at the front gate, but once he'd identified himself, was allowed entry. As he crossed the yard, he noted the police tape, but activity was nil. He walked into the main office hut to sign in.

'Thanks for coming in Jeremy. I want you to meet...' said Dan.

'Det.Sgt Brad Mallinson,' interjected Brad.

Jeremy shook his hand unemotionally. 'Is something the matter? All I was asked to do was come in.'

'We're trying to work that out now, Mr. Pyke,' said Brad.

'Jeremy will be fine.' He turned to Dan. 'What's going on, Dan?'

Dan retold the discovery of Vic's truck, how it was parked and all the facts relating to his possible disappearance.'

'Vic and Jack are missing?'

'We don't know that yet, but it certainly seems that way.'

'Does Dawn know?' asked Jeremy.

'Not yet,' explained Brad. 'That's part of the problem. It seemed she called him last night, she was having severe contractions. He never arrived at the hospital and in the process, Dawn lost the baby.'

Jeremy was visibly shaken by that news. 'Is she okay?'

'She will be,' said Brad. 'She's recovering but doesn't know about Vic yet and we'd appreciate it if you said nothing either.'

'Uhm, sure,' said Jeremy.

As Jeremy leant against the wall, the supervisor entered.

'What's up with the locker?' said Dan.

'There appears to be only one thing missing and I know they are because we haven't needed them for months.'

'What is it then?' asked Brad.

'D6 blasting caps.'

'Blasting caps are missing? Who'd want to take blasting caps?' queried Dan.

'We'll get what's still there dusted and we'll find out,' said Brad. He stepped outside and had forensics dust the blasting caps. The supervisor showed them where they were in the locker.

When they had been dusted, Brad had Jeremy open the explosives locker. Once open, the supervisor checked the inventory and reported that all explosives were present.

'Thanks for the assistance, Dan,' said Brad. 'I think we have all we need from the site, but I'd like the site to remain closed for at least the rest of the day.'

'As we've sent the men home, there'll be no calling them back.'

Brad smiled. 'I'll leave a constable on duty until I'm satisfied we don't need access to the site anymore. At that time, I will call you and let you know.'

'Do we have to keep someone from the company on site as well?' asked Dan.

'We'd only need one person,' said Brad. 'Could you roster yourselves?'

'I guess we can work something out,' said Dan. 'Are we going to be allowed to move about the site?'

'As long as you're careful and if you see anything unusual, that's not likely to be worksite related, inform the constable immediately and we'll come and check it out.'

'Understood.'

2.3

Crpl Jake North sat at his desk and began to sort through the case files he was working on. He glanced up to see a flashing message on his computer screen. Activating the message, he read with interest the report of some stolen D6 detonators, along with the disappearance of a Vic Forde and Jack DeVries.

Jake spied David crossing the room and greeted him accordingly.

'David, can you have a look at this?'

David leaned over Jake's shoulder and read the screen. He made all the usual grunts and even nodded his head a few times.

'What do you make of it?' asked Jake, when he saw that David had finished reading.

'There could be something in it,' replied David. 'Why are you getting this information?'

'After the D6 went missing back in January, I was curious to see if anyone decided to nick some blasting caps. Lo and behold, they have.'

'Could be coincidence?'

'Granted, but there are also two men missing. One is ex-military.'

As they discussed the matter, David could see LCmdr. Linda Barrow pacing about her office from the corner of his eye. He watched as she removed her earpiece, massaged her temples and opened her office door.

'David, can you come in here a minute, please?'

'Right away, Linda.'

David deposited his satchel and went into Linda's office, closing the door behind him. Jake continued to read the police report and jumped when he heard his name being called. He stood and saw David waving for him to join them in Linda's office. He crossed the floor and walked in.

'Firstly, I want to congratulate you on a wonderful job you've been doing since you joined us back in January,' said Linda.

'Thanks, Ma'am,' replied Jake.

'David tells me that you're still monitoring a case from the day you started? The one where two soldiers went missing delivering D6 back to Williams.'

'That's right and just today I received info from an alert I'd set up that some D6 blasting caps were stolen from a worksite in the inner west the other night.'

'Yes, David mentioned that too,' said Linda. 'I want you to get all the details you can.'

'Did he mention that two people are allegedly missing?' said Jake.

'Yes, but no names,' said Linda. 'Do you have names?'

'I read further into the report and they are listing the names as a Vic Forde and a Jack DeVries.'

Linda visibly slumped in her chair.

'Is everything okay, Ma'am?' asked David.

'Vic Forde was the CO of my army unit when we were

deployed overseas about ten years ago. Unfortunately, he was injured in action and soon afterwards the whole unit returned home, were offered redeployment or discharge. All but three retired from the Army. One of the other unit members was Damian Smithson.'

Jake's eyebrows rose at the mention of his name. 'He is one of the men missing from the D6 situation in January.'

'Yes, he is, and we still don't know anything,' said Linda.

'What would you like me to do?' said Jake.

'As you have just said, D6 blasting caps have been stolen. I daresay we have nothing to link this episode with the one back in January, but until that is absolutely clear, I want them to be treated as if they were related. Think outside the square, and I don't mean by a little bit. Anything that has any connection is to be included and investigated. David, if you need to bring anyone else into the group, you have my authority to do so as required, just keep me in the loop.'

'Yes, Ma'am,' Jake and David replied.

'Dismissed.'

Both men stood, left Linda's office and went to Jake's desk.

'I'll make sure you have the access you need to the Glass,' said David.

'The "Glass"?' asked Jake.

'Haven't you used it yet?'

Jake shook his head.

'We need to bring you up to speed then. It's the sophisticated glass table top and projector we use to display, scan, cross-ref and collate any data we have for a case. I reckon you'll need it for this one.'

Before going back to their desks, David directed Jake to the room where the 'Glass' was kept.

The 'Glass' room was one without windows. In the middle and towards one wall was a large table with a slightly tilted glass top. Jake was suitably impressed.

'Initial activation is here,' said David, pressing an area on the lower right corner of the table.

The table top lit up. Jake could now see that the top was in fact a large screen.

'It can be used manually, by typing on the screen, speaking to it or downloading data from a connected tablet,' added David.

'silly question,' said Jake, 'But does the table have a name?'

'Ask it?'

David stepped back.

'Good morning,' said Jake tentatively.

'Good morning,' responded the table. 'Please state your name and rank. I do not recognise the voice.'

Jake looked over at David, who was grinning.

'You're enjoying this, aren't you?'

David made the action of zipping his lips.

'Right then.' Jake stood straighter, took a deep breath and continued. 'I am Crpl Jake North and I wish to be registered with the glass top table.'

'Thank you, Crpl North,' responded the table.

"You may refer to me as, Jake. Do you have a name?'

'I am Interactive Glass Table 2020, or IGT20.' The glass top flashed up with the name.

'That's not a name I want to call every time,' said Jake.

'Do you have a better name, Jake?'

'Give me a moment, I'm thinking.' Jake walked back and forth in front of the table looking at the words. He stopped and smiled. 'Lassie. I name you Lassie.'

'You're naming me after a fictional animal character from a television show?'

'It does happen to be the same, but no. I've taken the last four letters from the word glass and named you that way.'

'Accepted.'

'Excellent. Hello, Lassie.'

'Hello, Jake.'

David chuckled and left Jake to get used to the device.

When Jake felt comfortable enough using it, he turned towards his desk. As he crossed the room, he saw Linda leaving David's desk.

David called Jake over to his desk.

'Linda just informed me that the Police department will be sending a man over on Monday to liaise with us on this case,' said David.

'Did they explain why?'

'One of the missing men from the worksite case is ex-military. They felt we should be involved.'

'Have they been told about the missing D6 and the direct military connection?' asked Jake.

'No, Linda didn't mention it.'

'What else did Linda say?'

'That we are to give them every DFIS hospitality,' said David.

'That sounds like we should give them a damned hard time?'

David laughed. 'Not quite, we just simply let them know who's running the operation. In this case, that would be you.'

Jake baulked slightly. 'Me? I thought you were the lead?'

'Technically I am, but as to the grunt work, that's you. If you need help with the investigation, you ask and I'll supply.'

Jake walked directly to his desk the following Monday morning. He dropped his satchel, retrieved his tablet and went to the Glass. The information he'd entered on Friday was all there. Dates, pictures, forensics results, names; all the information relating to the theft of the D6 in January and the disappearance of the two soldiers. Even the discovery of the playing and sunflower cards was shown.

As he stood and pondered all the details, his remote earpiece activated.

'Corporal North, a Det. Anhton Roberts to see you, sir.'

'I'll be right down,' he said and disconnected the call.

Jake stood calmly in the lift as he travelled to the ground floor. As he stepped from the lift, he spotted Det. Roberts standing by the reception desk. Crossing the floor, Jake met the extremely firm grip of Anhton's handshake.

'It's good to meet you, Det. Roberts,' said Jake.

'Likewise, Crpl North,' said Anhton, smiling.

'Jake is fine,' added Jake. 'This way, please,' added Jake, indicating the lift.

'I can handle that. Anhton's fine with me too,' he said, relaxing only slightly.

'How are you providing the data for us?' asked Jake.

'Electronically.'

Jake nodded. The lift stopped, and Jake showed Anhton to the room where the Glass was. Within a matter of minutes, all the information relating to the detonators' theft and the men's disappearances was loaded. Jake also made sure that Anhton's tablet was linked to the Glass for the case file only.

'Let's see what we have,' said Jake, rearranging the information. 'What can we deal with quickly, Anhton?'

'I reckon the easiest is going to be the black paper parasol, and the cards,' he replied. 'Forensics found nothing unusual on them or about them. Standard products used. The team even found some of the same items in a craft store. There were no fingerprints of note on them anywhere.'

'Not even from those who made the thing?'

'There were some of those, but only partials. Nothing we could work with, but they have been recorded all the same. Our guys reckon the prints have been there for quite a long time.'

'I will file that with the sunflower card,' said Jake. 'Then we have the playing card. It matches the one from the first crime scene and I reckon they're from the same deck.'

'You think so?' asked Anhton.

'We'll keep checking. What about the blasting caps?'

'Nothing of note there. There were some fingerprints, but they've all been accounted for.'

Anhton indicated the prints of the four people who had access to the locker and then those of Vic and another man, a Jeremy Pyke, who had authority to access the explosives locker inside. Anhton also showed Jake the data that had been recovered of who'd accessed the locks to both the locker and the explosives locker inside. The dates and times matched normal usage and nothing showed up as having been accessed at the approximate time when the incidents took place.

'Not much there for the moment. Any trace yet of Vic Forde or Jack DeVries?'

'Nothing. We've heard nothing from Jack and Vic still hasn't come home, nor has been in contact with Dawn either.'

'That would be his partner, Dawn Forde?'

'Yeah, Det.Snr.Sgt Dawn Forde.'

'Have you heard how she is, by the way?'

'She's doing as well as can be expected.'

Jake began stroking his chin in thought. He moved bits of information around, then moved some back again when Anhton indicated their relevancy to other pieces of information. They both jumped slightly when a knock came on the glass wall separating the main office from the Glass room.

Jake turned to see Linda standing there.

'Hi Linda, this is Det. Anhton Roberts,' said Jake. 'Anhton, this is LCmdr Linda Barrow.'

They shook hands.

'Any more news?' asked Linda.

'Nothing new yet, Ma'am,' said Jake.

Linda stood and looked at the table where the information was shown. 'I see you have Jeremy Pyke's name there as well now?'

'Do you know him?' asked Jake.

'He was in the same Army unit with me,' she replied.

'Is that the same one as...' Jake paused, sifting through data on the screen, 'Vic Forde?'

'Along with Damian?' said Linda

'Who else was in your unit?' asked Jake.

'Let's see,' replied Linda, staring off into the distance.

'There was Peter Dugald, Derik Scott, Garthen Todorovic, Danika Wordsworth, Vienata Grond-Fiala, Giulia Quinn, Damian, Vic, Jeremy and me. Yes, ten of us.'

'How long ago was this?'

'About ten years. We were only together a short time.'

'I didn't think women served on the frontline back then,' said Jake.

'We weren't exactly on the frontline, but we were also the first mixed unit as close as possible to active combat.'

'How come you weren't together long?'

'It was about two years, so we'd come to know each other very well. Anyway, we were on a patrol close to our base when an unauthorised local vehicle came barrelling towards us. We ordered it to stop, but it refused. We fired several shots at it, eventually shooting out its tyres, but it continued. Then it opened fired on us. Vic, Damian and Jeremy were forced to one side of the road, whilst the rest of us took cover on the opposite side. It veered towards us and we retreated. We found better cover and as we did the truck exploded. In the ensuing confusion, we were herded back to base, insisting that our colleagues were still out there. When someone finally listened to us, and allowed us to leave base, we found Damian and Jeremy dragging Vic between them. We grabbed a stretcher, ran out to them, laid Vic on it and carried him back to base. We got him to the medics and whilst he survived, he wasn't going to be able to walk properly again. For some reason, all Jeremy could think about was that we'd abandoned them. He refused to listen. We were told that it was probably the trauma. Six months later we were shipped back to Australia and we disbanded. I chose to stay in the Army and moved into the Military Police, earning my way to DFIS a couple of years ago. As to what everyone else did, I never found out, until more recently. Danika is now the president-elect of the new Basslea Republic, Peter has become the base commander at Williams, and is married to Danika, Vienata is in the opposing political party to Danika and Giulia is Danika's personal assistant. That's about it, I think.'

'That is certainly quite a bit. Thanks, Linda,' said Jake.

'It's very interesting indeed,' added Anhton.

'I hope I've been able to help,' said Linda. 'Make sure you keep me in the loop, Jake. If my old army unit is involved, I want to know.'

'I will, Linda,' said Jake.

Linda left the room and Jake added the last bit of information into the file. 'What do you think, Anhton?'

'I'm not sure at present, but it's worth keeping note that so many people involved in this case were in the same Army unit together ten years ago.'

'That is rather a coincidence but may have nothing to do with it at all,' said Jake. 'Do you think it's worth chatting to the remaining unit members to see what they know?'

'I think all we'd find out is what happened ten years ago, with slightly different viewpoints. Not that relevant right now though,' said Anhton.

'True, well we have the info now, so we can go back to it if we need to.'

Jake and Anhton spent the rest of the morning collating the info they had. They exhausted all the leads the Police had and when it turned four, they called it quits for the day.

2.4

Jake came home from the meeting with Anhton with his head full. As was his practice, Jake showered and changed. Today he decided to use aroma oils in his time of meditation.

Clearing a space in the middle of the lounge, the scents filling the air, he started to play one of his meditation tracks. Sitting on a cushion, he crossed his legs and chanted quietly until he found himself sitting on the bank of a lake, that was one of his favourites as a child.

- Vic Forde and Jack DeVries missing,

- No trace at all, similar to soldiers,

- D6 blasting caps taken,

- Could be used in conjunction with stolen D6 from January,

- Intervening period is too long,

- Discovery of military links,

- Ex-members currently high-profile positions with new republic,

- No apparent links between missing soldiers and missing workmen,

- Must watch link with Danika Wordsworth,

- Use Linda Barrow more,

Jake's meditation was suddenly interrupted by his phone telling him his mother was calling.

'Hello, mum ... yes, I'm looking after myself ... I know it's been a while since I came to visit ... no mum ... you'll be the first to know, mum ... yes, the plants you gave me are still alive ... actually, I'd love you to come over some time and help with some trees in the back-yard ... okay, bye ... love you too.'

3.1

The dark utility pulled into the car park as the sun went down. When fully dark, a black clad figure got out of the utility. Walking to the edge of a building, the shadows afforded the now crouching figure the cover desired. A backpack was placed on the ground and a set of night vision goggles retrieved. Not specifically needed, as the target building opposite had adequate lighting, but with the distance across the road being far enough, the goggles allowed for clarity.

At 8:25pm, the dark figure light-footedly dashed across the road. Hiding in the shadow of a large dump bin, the figure waited. At 8:30, the man who owned "Blasted Leads" opened the rear door and exited carrying a box to his car. Whilst the man's back was turned, the dark figure crept inside the warehouse, noted the matching alarm keypad inside the door and found a place to hide.

The owner of the business came and went four times and eventually locked and alarmed the building. Waiting quietly for ten minutes, the figure crept from his hiding place, walked over to the alarm and disarmed it. Moving quickly, the desired bundles of fuse lead were located and four five-metre rolls were stowed in the backpack. Making sure the remainder looked like nothing had happened, the figure opened the door slowly, made sure no one was about, left the building and set the alarm again.

Walking quickly across the road, the figure tossed the backpack into the passenger seat of the black utility and drove away. It wasn't until the ute was merging with traffic on the major road that the lights were switched on.

3.2

Rick Ourdetall looked at the mobile phone dancing around on the table in front of him. A sigh of frustration escaped his lips, before silencing it with another mouthful of his dinner.

'What's the matter, dear?' asked his wife.

'I can't even eat in peace without the phone going off,' he replied.

It kept ringing and eventually it stopped.

'There, they gave up,' he said.

It rang again.

'I'll answer it for you and tell them you're not available,' said his wife.

Rick shrugged his shoulders. 'You'll only have to give it to me.'

His wife answered the phone. 'Blasted Leads, this is Stacey, how can I help you? ... I see ... he's having his dinner right now, is it important?'

Rick looked at his wife with surprise and concern. 'What's the matter?'

'I'll let him know, one moment please.' Stacey pressed a button on the smartphone. 'It's the security company. Did you go back to the shop tonight? After you left at about 8:45?'

'No, why?'

'You'd better speak to them then. The alarm was turned off ten minutes after you left and turned back on about seven and a half minutes after that.'

Rick reached for the phone. 'Rick Ourdetall here ... that's correct ... no I didn't ... yes, that might be a wise thing to do ... I'll meet you there in about thirty minutes.' Rick put the phone on the table. 'They think there may have been a break-in.'

'Will you want anything to eat when you get home later?'

'I'll be right, hon. I have no idea how long I'll be.' Rick finished his dinner, got up and kissed his wife, grabbed the phone and left.

As Rick travelled to the store, he tried to slow his breathing, trying not to panic. He couldn't think properly. What was the damage going to be? Even if something had been stolen, he told himself calmly, hopefully the insurance company would to cover it. He arrived at his warehouse store in twenty minutes. Waiting for him was a car from the security company. Rick got out of his car and approached the rear door. As he did, the security guard also approached the door.

'Good evening, Mr Ourdetall. Let's hope it was a malfunctioning alarm pad and nothing more,' said the guard.

'It's only been installed a few years, it shouldn't be playing up just yet, ' said Rick.

The security guard smiled.

Rick approached the door and keyed the code to disarm the system. The panel glowed green and Rick went to unlock the door. 'It's already unlocked. The only way that can happen is for someone to have unlocked it from the inside before leaving. Unless they had a key, they could set the alarm but not lock the door. I don't like this now.'

'Then before you go any further, you should call the police,' said the guard. 'I'll stay until they arrive. I can then give them the information we have from our network.'

'Thanks,' said Rick. He pulled his phone from his pocket and dialled the police. He turned to the guard. 'Someone should be here soon.'

The guard nodded and radioed his base saying he'd be staying until the police no longer needed his assistance.

Rick was pacing around his car when the police arrived. Still, he jumped when the car pulled to a stop. He walked in their direction as they got out of the car. 'I'm glad you could come so quickly. I'm Rick Ourdetall, owner of Blasted Leads. I really want to get inside and see if anything's been taken, but the security guard advised I should wait.'

'Hello, Mr Ourdetall. Yes, it was wise of you to wait for us. I'm Det.Sgt Jared Hood and this is Const. Rithika Banner,' said the first police officer. 'What can you tell me?'

'Probably the security guard can tell you more as to what may have happened,' said Rick. 'They rang me when the alarm went off, which was only minutes after I'd left the premises.'

The police officer turned his attention to the security guard. 'What can you tell me?'

He pulled a smartphone from his pocket and pulled up a file. 'At 8:47 this evening, we recorded the alarm being set at 'Blasted Leads'. At 8:57, we recorded the alarm being de-activated and then at 9:03 the alarm was reset. I can give you exact seconds, if you want?'

'That's fine, thank you' said Jared. 'Are you able to pro-vide a copy of that file if required?'

'With clearance from Head Office, sure.'

Jared turned back to Rick. 'What can you add to this, Mr Ourdetall?'

'Well, when I arrived, the security guard was waiting,' he started. 'I then went to unlock the door, but it was already unlocked. I know I locked it when I left. I always make sure it's locked.'

'Could you have forgotten tonight? We're you distract-ed at all?'

'No,' insisted Rick. 'I make sure every night that the door is locked and the alarm set.'

'Okay. What happened next?'

'Nothing. The security guard recommended I call you. We haven't been inside yet, so I don't know if anything has been stolen?'

'Could the alarm system have malfunctioned?'

'I'm sure it hasn't, but I will be talking about that with the security company anyway. They suggested the same thing,' said Rick. 'Can we go inside yet? I need to make sure everything is there.'

'Okay, we'll go carefully,' said Jared.

Rick led the way. Jared advised the use of a handkerchief to handle the doors so as not to spoil potential fingerprints. The security guard remained outside and the two police officers followed Rick inside. Rick turned on the lights and once lighting was good, he began to move about. The police officers stayed near the door.

'Can you notice anything missing?' asked Jared.

'Nothing yet,' replied Rick, as he moved amongst the shelves. 'Everything seems to be oka...'

'Is there a problem, Mr Ourdetall?'

'Yes. Yes, something is missing. Four rolls of electric fuse wire. Each roll is five metres long. I know they were here today as a resupply only arrived yesterday and I put everything away myself.'

'What type of fuse is this wire used for?'

'A slapper fuse.'

Jared nodded. 'What are they used for?'

'Anything really, but mostly explosives.'

'I see,' said Jared.

'Can this be sorted tonight?' asked Rick, facing Jared. 'I can't afford to be shut tomorrow.'

'I'll see if someone can come out tonight, but if not, it will have to wait until the morning.'

Rick wasn't happy.

'I appreciate the inconvenience that this may cause, but if forensics can't make it out until tomorrow, then there is nothing we can do.' Jared turned to the officer that was with him. 'I'm going to make a call. Make sure he doesn't move anything about. I need forensics to look at the place as it is.'

The officer nodded.

Jared picked up his phone and dialled a number. 'Anhton, I hope I haven't caught you at a bad time?'

'Nah, it's fine. As exciting as my life is, I thought might go to bed early,' said Anhton.

'Not tonight. I'm here at a company on the edge of Essendon airport and some slapper leads have been supposedly stolen. Well, according to the owner they have.'

Jared went on to explain the deal with the alarms going on and off, possibly from the inside.

'Why would you tell me?' asked Anhton.

'One of the uses for a slapper fuse is with explosives.'

'Really? Not only do we have someone with some stolen D6 and blasting caps, but now we have someone with fuse wire.'

'Can you get forensics over here?' said Jared. 'I think this should be handled by you.'

'You might be right. I'll see if I can arrange someone for tonight.'

Jared disconnected the call and went back inside.

'There should be someone here tonight,' said Jared. 'You will most likely have to stay out of the way. We'll stay here until they arrive, then they will give the all clear to lock up when they're done.'

'How long do I have to wait?' said Rick impatiently.

'As long as you have to,' said Jared.

Jake and Amy from DFIS forensics arrived and were shown the rear door.

'Amy, can you do the door and the alarm pads whilst I have a look inside?' said Jake.

'Sure,' said Amy.

Jake turned when he heard another car arrive. Anhton stepped out and walked the short distance to where Jake was.

'Hello, Jake,' said Anhton.

'Hi, Anhton, what brings you here?' said Jake.

'I know I don't have to be here, but as I was the one who passed on the message, I thought I'd come to see if I could help.'

'You can help me inside.'

'Deal,' said Anhton.

Jake and Anhton carefully moved into the warehouse storeroom.

'What are we looking for?' asked Anhton.

'Anything out of the ordinary,' said Jake.

'Like?'

'If someone was inside and unseen when the door was alarmed, where did they hide?'

'What about under here?' said Anhton, indicating a space under one of the desks.

'Where's the owner?' called Jake.

'I'm right here,' came the reply.

'Crpl Jake North, DFIS, and this is Det. Anhton Roberts.'

'Metro North,' added Anhton.

'Rick Ourdetall, owner.'

'Mr Ourdetall, would you have seen anyone hiding under this desk as you moved about?' said Jake, indicating the space under the desk in question.

'If I was concentrating on my boxes, then I probably wouldn't. especially if I wasn't expecting anyone to be there.'

'Thank you. If you could wait outside again.'

Rick nodded and stepped back outside.

Jake crawled into the space and pressed himself as far back as he could. 'Anhton, can you walk past a few times at a normal distance carrying a box?'

Anhton obliged and after walking back and forth a few times, he replaced the box and helped Jake to his feet.

'Trying to forget I was there, did you see me as you passed by?'

Anhton screwed up his face. 'No, I cannot recall seeing you hidden there.'

'Now, if the lights were low and the figure was dressed in dark clothes, someone could have easily blended into the shadows. Correct?'

'Sounds plausible.'

'We need to get Rick to see if anything is missing,' said Jake. 'Mr Ourdetall, can you come back inside please?'

'How can I help now?' said Rick, looking a little weary.

'I need you to show me the shelves where the stock was taken.'

'This way,' said Rick.

Jake and Anhton followed him. he walked to the third row and stopped about halfway along.

'Here. There are four five-metre rolls of slapper fuse wire missing,' said Rick.

'Can you explain to me what exactly slapper fuse is?' asked Jake.

As Jake spoke with Rick, Anhton moved along the shelves.

Anhton could hear Rick explaining some details. He shone his torch along a shelf when it reflected of something. Moving closer he discovered a small glass bottle.

'Jake, you may want to have a look at this,' he called.

Jake turned and he and Rick moved to Anhton's side.

'Is this yours. Mr Ourdetall?' asked Anhton.

Rick leant in and looked at the bottle.

'Not anything I'd have out here and I have no idea how it would've got there. It looks like an old ink bottle to me.'

'Thank you, Mr Ourdetall,' said Anhton.

'If you could wait outside again please Mr Ourdetall, I need to do my job now.'

Jake fetched his kit and began by photographing the position of the bottle on the shelf before carefully removing it and bagging it. Underneath the bottle, they found another playing card.

Jake dusted for prints around the location of the bottle and then around the shelves where the rolls of wire were taken. After consulting with Amy, Jake was satisfied that they had everything they needed.

'We're done here,' said Jake. 'Mr. Ourdetall, you may lock up your warehouse now.'

'It's about time too,' said Rick and left to lock up.

'He's a cheery one then,' said Amy.

'It's understandable. His warehouse has been accessed without his knowledge, items taken, and he's been kept here waiting for us to finish for an hour,' said Jake. 'I think I'd be a bit irritable too.'

'I guess so,' said Amy.

'Anyway, we need to get this stuff back to the lab. Gabby has work to do for us in the morning,' said Jake.

'I guess that means I'm heading out too,' said Anhton.

'Unless you want to sleep in your car overnight, I would think so,' said Jake.

Anhton smiled wryly at Jake.

'Goodnight, corporal.

'Good night, detective.'

Jake and Amy climbed into their van and followed Anhton out of the carpark.

3.3

Rick stood behind the counter of his store the day after the robbery. He turned and stared through the wall at the rough position where the stock was taken from. He pulled out his phone and dialled a number. He walked into his office as it rang.

'Calderwood Industries, how may I direct you call?'

'Hello. Can I speak to Ms. M please?'

'One moment.'

Rick heard the distinctive tones of the call being transferred, then he heard a click, white noise and then another click.

'This is Ms. M.'

'Rick O here.'

'What can I do for you, Rick O?'

'Has your lot decided to rob me? If you needed supplies, all you had to do was ask.'

'I can assure you, Rick O, we do not steal from our own.'

'Well, I was robbed last night. Someone took some slapper leads.'

'It wasn't us. We know that if we need some, we will place a legitimate order through appropriate channels. Is that all?'

'Yes it is.'

The call as terminated.

Rick went back to fussing about in his store.

* * * * *

Ms. M sat at her desk and pondered the conversation. She picked up her phone and dialled a number.

'Yes?' said the voice.

'Have you gone behind my back and ordered a theft from one of our operatives?' asked Ms. M.

'Why would I do that?'

'I'm only asking.'

'Do you think that I would keep you out of the loop?' said the voice.

'Not at all.'

'Very good. You are my closest confidant. Whist I make the decisions, you always know what they will be..'

'I understand,' said Ms M.

'Do you have anything else to report?'

Ms. M was silent.

'I thought not,' said the voice and terminated the call.

3·4

Anhton parked his car outside DFIS HQ and wandered inside. He checked in and rode the lift to Jake's level. He exited and crossed the floor, spotting Jake as he did.

'Morning, Jake,' he called.

'Ah, morning, Anhton,' said Jake.

'Does Gabby have anything yet?'

Jake sat down and accessed his mail. 'Nothing yet. Give it time, she's probably only just seen the pile on her desk.' At that moment, Jake's terminal began to buzz. Jake turned to Anhton, 'This is her now.' Jake turned back to the screen and activated the video call. 'Good morning, my precious.'

'Don't you good morning me, mister,' said Gabby, holding up the samples. 'You know I have a lot on right now and you put these samples right in the middle of my desk.'

'Yes I did, and you love me for it.'

'Don't give me that sweet shit.'

'Language, please, we have a guest,' said Jake.

Anhton stood behind Jake. 'Hi, Gabby, I'm Det. Anhton Roberts.'

'Hi, sweetie, I've heard about you,' said Gabby. 'Sorry about my language.'

'What have you been told about me?' asked Anhton.

'No need to answer that,' interrupted Jake. 'Can you have a look at those samples for me today, Gab? I need the results by tonight.'

'Only because you have company and I can't swear in front of someone I don't really know, I have no choice.'

'Thank you. I'll be down later,' said Jake.

'You'd better, young man. We have things to talk about.' Gabby terminated the call.

'What have you been saying to her about me?' asked Anhton.

'Only that I was working with you,' said Jake, trying to not to look at Anhton.

Anhton stood up and moved away from Jake's chair.

'As Linda said to us after the blasting caps, everything, every little thing, is to be counted until proven otherwise. This counts. Do you want to run it up on the Glass?'

'I'd love a go at that thing.' Anhton made sure he had a copy of the reports on his tablet, walked over to the Glass, and loaded the new data. It was cross-referenced wherever possible but nothing new appeared.

'Anything else we need to add?' asked Anhton.

'Well, being primarily military, I've been following up on the army unit that Linda mentioned,' said Jake. He loaded the file he'd created and soon Anhton saw all the info available. 'As you can see, I've added more detail as to who's doing what nowadays.'

'What Linda said about Danika, Vienata, Peter and Giulia is correct. We already know what Damian was doing. Now we know the rest,' said Anhton, looking over the list on the screen.

'Jeremy is in construction, and we know he sometimes worked with Vic. Derik is a news reporter.'

'I know him. At least I've seen him on the news. He specialises in politics and military reporting.'

'Yes, I thought I recognised the name. Then there's Garthen Todorovic. He's a security guard in Heidelberg.'

'An army unit of ten who were quite close at the time of the accident,' surmised Anhton. 'Perhaps you could try to find out why they were disbanded. It seems odd to me that after only being together for two years that they were disbanded after the injury of their commander. There must've been something else with that, don't you think?'

'I'll try, but I know how hard it can be to get that type of info.'

'If anyone can, you'll be best suited.'

'Granted. I can ask.' Jake made a note on his tablet to investigate.

David strode into the room. 'What's this about blasting leads being stolen? Talk to me, Jake.'

'Look at the Glass, sir, and I'll explain.' Jake stood upright, having assessed David's professional stance. Jake showed David the info they had processed from the night before. Anhton even took a turn to explain what he'd seen.

'This is getting serious,' exclaimed David, sternly. 'We need some answers. What's being done? Do we need more help?'

'I can follow up on the police investigations, sir,' said Anhton. 'I'll have the best access to files and personnel.'

'Done. Jake?'

'I'll go over the forensics of the army truck and see if there's anything we've missed. Also, I'm going to follow-up on a potential lead concerning the number of people attached to the same army unit and their association with this case.'

'Sparse but do it anyway. Linda wants an update. Call in more help if you need to, Jake.'

'Okay. Did you know Linda was in the same army unit?'

'Isn't that a little too close to home?' asked David.

'We'll find out in due course, but she might have info that we could get no other way.'

'All right, but tread carefully.'

'I always do,' said Jake.

'Get to it then,' said David and left as abruptly as he arrived.

'What's eating him?' asked Anhton.

'Nothing, it's the way he gets now and then. He's very officious when he wants or needs to be. As he said, Linda wants an update. He's just making sure we're not slacking off and that we give him what he wants ASAP.'

'I'd better get going then,' said Anhton.

'Sounds good. Send me anything you have so I can add it to the file.'

'Will do.' Anhton collected his briefcase and left the office.

Jake left the Glass room and walked to his desk. Halfway along he looked up and saw Linda. Diverting, he went to her office. He knocked lightly on her door.

She called him in and offered him a seat.

'How can I help you, Jake?'

'I was wondering if I might be able to ask you about the army unit?' said Jake a little gingerly.

'Don't be shy. Are we suspects?'

'No, not suspects, but two of the unit have been supposedly killed in recent times, one whilst on duty, the other for doing his job.'

'This is true,' said Linda. 'What do you want to know?'

'Why was the unit disbanded?'

There was a moment silence. Linda rose and looked out her window.

'I've done it now,' thought Jake.

After a few minutes, she sat back down.

'After the incident I told you about, we were debriefed as a group and individually. No one was to blame, but Jeremy seemed to become slightly more isolated. He spent as much time as he could with Vic until he was sent home. Once he was gone, it was as much a mutual decision as it was commands that we should also return home. For the entire trip home, we all sat with our own thoughts. Once back in Australia we were assessed and given options. As you know, some of us stayed with the military but moved to new areas. Whilst others chose to take honourable discharges and pursue other avenues. Being an MP and then DFIS, I became privy to slightly more information. Unless it becomes absolutely necessary, that information stays with me.'

'I understand that.'

'Why are you interested in the army unit?'

'Whilst on the very edge, it has popped up in two of the three incidents we've investigated so far. Some would say that's coincidental. I'd rather rule it out than have it become something of concern and we had missed it for too long.'

'Anytime you need help, let me know.'

Jake thanked Linda for her time and went back to his desk to update the information he had.

3.5

Jake went from his DFIS desk to the gym. He met An-hton there and after they'd changed and warmed up on a treadmill, they began a stretching regime. Anhton asked if he might have a copy of Jake's routine, as he liked what he saw.

'Do you mean me or my routine?' asked Jake.

This caught Anhton off-guard and he turned bright red.

'It's okay, Anhton, both are fine with me.'

Anhton took a moment to register what Jake had said, but when he did, he beamed.

Jake prepared to push some weights and with his music playing, he thought about his day.

- Four men missing, 2 soldiers and 2 civilians,

- One civilian ex-army,

- Blasting leads stolen,

- Blasting caps and D6 also stolen,

- What relationship does the army unit have?

- Will Linda be a help or hindrance?

- Jake changed equipment and resumed his thought process;

- Must expand alerts,

- Have I missed anything with forensics?

- Review police report for robbery at Blasted Leads.

- Check times alarm was switched on and off,

- Talk to owner to find out his routine that night.

Jake and Anhton finished the rest of their workouts and were leaving the change rooms when Jake walked into another gym member, for which he made apologies. 'I definitely need to speak to the owner of Blasted Leads about what he was doing that night,' he said aloud.

4.1

Garthen Todorovich arrived at Redberg Electronics at nine pm. He parked his security company car and walked to the rear entrance of the small suburban warehouse. He swiped his card and entered the warehouse.

'Evening, Tony,' said Garthen, dropping his bag on the end of the desk.

'Hey, Garthen,' said Tony.

'Much happening tonight?'

'Some of the staff are still here. You might want to pop your head in to let them know you're here.'

'Will do.'

Tony swiped his security pass and logged off. Garthen did the same and logged on.

'See ya tomorrow, Garthen.'

'Will do, Tony.'

Tony left and Garthen took a quick stroll around the building. He spoke with the remaining staff, who were just packing up when he arrived.

'What are these for?' asked Garthen, as he helped stow some small containers in a storage cupboard.

'These are the new master access cards and security codes for the Forden AVs being released,' said the technician, locking the cupboard, and then dropping the key into the top drawer of a nearby desk.

'No more keys,' said Garthen.

'There hasn't been for a few years, but these new designs should be a little more secure than previous ones.'

'I'm sure the drivers will be pleased about that. Too many cars are being stolen again.'

'You have a good night, Garthen, and look after these codes for me,' said the tech, picking up his bag and leaving the room.

'Night,' said Garthen. He switched off the light and continued his routine first check of the building. When he was happy, he returned to the security desk and took out his tablet to read the news.

At 00:15am, Garthen stepped outside for a smoke, and to check the outside of the building. He usually left the door unlocked, as he was only away five minutes, but this time he closed it completely.

The door was located on the side of the building, at the end of some parking spaces. Bordering the parking spaces, was a waist-high hedge. There was space near the wall of the building for someone to walk through.

Laying very low behind the hedge, a dark figure watched as Garthen walked towards the door. Hearing Garthen rattle around for his keycard, the figure moved to a crouching position. As the door opening, the figure jumped over the hedge and grabbed Garthen from behind.

Garthen felt something press into his back. He took a sharp breath and stiffened. He didn't dare move.

'Inside,' said the gruff voice. 'Main desk, now!'

Garthen resisted but was hit over the head, drawing a small amount of blood that trickled down his neck. He relented and led his assailant to the main security desk. At gunpoint, Garthen was forced to sit.

'Disarm everything!'

Garthen began to disarm the alarm system.

'Cameras too!'

Garthen complied.

Just then the phone on the security desk began to ring.

If I don't answer, they'll know something is wrong and will send help, Garthen thought.

The phone rang out.

Garthen relaxed slightly.

The phone began to ring again.

'Answer it!' ordered the figure.

With the gun only millimetres from his head, he picked up the phone.

'Todorovich,' said Garthen.

'What's going on over there?'

Garthen looked at his assailant.

'We've got a bit of a problem here,' said Garthen.

'Do you need assistance?'

The gun was now resting against his temple. Garthen began to sweat. *What am I going to say?*

The gun pressed further into his temple.

'I'm fine. We seem to have some electrical surge. I'm waiting for the system to reset.'

'Are you sure? We can send a tech out to investigate.'

'No. If it gets worse, I'll call back.'

Garthen terminated the call.

'Where are the keycards kept?'

'I don't know,' replied Garthen.

'Show me where they are. NOW!'

Garthen flinched at the menace in the voice. He rose and led the figure to the storage room.

'Open the locker!'

Garthen didn't wait to be told a second time and re-trieved the key from the top drawer of the desk. He opened the locker and stood back.

'Which containers are they?'

'I don't know, I don't work here,' said Garthen.

'Open each one until I say stop!'

One by one, Garthen removed the containers until the one containing the current cards was opened.

'That one, close it and place it in the backpack.' A back-pack was placed on the desk and Garthen dropped the con-tainer into it.

'Keep going!'

Garthen opened the remainder of the containers; three more were dropped into the backpack.

'Re-lock the locker.'

When that was done, Garthen was taken back to secu-rity station and told to restart the system with a five-minute delay. With the threat of another blow to the head, he did as he was told.

'I think I know your voice,' said Garthen, turning to look at the figure. As he turned, a needle was plunged into his neck and he collapsed onto the desk unconscious.

The figure left the building, threw the backpack over his shoulders and proceeded to disable the external lighting. Jogging lightly through the shadows to a matt-black ute a few streets away, the backpack was stowed behind the front seat. Driving the vehicle, the figure returned to the small warehouse and backed up to the door. Re-entering the building, the inert body of Garthen was removed.

The body was injected once more, wrapped in plastic, and loaded onto the back of the matte-black ute. Driving a few streets before turning on lights, the ute was driven across town to a warehouse in the inner west of Melbourne where it pulled into the basement and parked.

Garthen's lifeless body was packed into a drum and covered with a green liquid. The backpack was taken from behind the seat of the ute and the small containers holding the access cards and codes were secured in a storage locker in one corner.

Moving to a small cot, the figure rested. After a couple of hours, the body in the drum was inspected. The drum was lifted into place on the press. A heavy disc was placed on top and the press activated. When complete, it was sealed and placed on the back of another utility beside the four other drums.

A door in the far left corner opened and closed.

4.2

At seven am, the day shift security guard arrived. He discovered that the side door had been left open. He did a quick check of the outside of the building. Upon entering, he couldn't find Garthen anywhere. He searched the whole building carefully but could see nothing wrong. He called back to base to find out if they knew what happened to Garthen. He was told that the systems had been off-line for thirty minutes and that the base was told by Garthen there had been a power surge during the night.

At eight thirty, the first of the Redberg staff arrived. The guard informed them that the night guard was nowhere to be found and that the side door had been left open.

'Do we call the police or not?' said one technician.

'I don't think that's necessary just yet,' replied the guard. 'I'd like you to carefully go through the building, touching as little as possible and if you have to touch, use gloves.'

The three staff allowed to enter the building nodded their heads and went inside.

Other staff began to arrive and were barred from entering the building.

An hour later, the three allowed inside appeared at the side door.

'What did you find?' asked the guard.

'It's what we didn't find that's alarming,' said a technician.

'Ok, what didn't you find?' said the guard.

'The last room we checked was where we keep the secure storage lockers. When we opened them we found that some of the containers holding the new master Forden AV access cards and codes were missing,' explained the technician.

'Can they be tracked?' asked the guard.

'They haven't been activated properly, but they can be used,' said the tech.

'What do you mean?'

'Well, if someone who is smart enough knows how to read them and the codes, they can set the cards to open any Forden AV that has the current software.'

'I see,' said the guard. 'I think now is the right time to call the police.'

As the security guard finished his call to the police, the general manager of the electronics company arrived. The guard spotted the suited woman approach the building and intercepted her before she could enter.

'I'm sorry, Ma'am, but I cannot let anyone enter the building,' he explained politely.

'What's going on, Matt?' she said, turning to the tech who had explained to the guard about the missing containers.

He quickly re-told what he knew. The general manager turned back to the guard.

'Can we at least wait in our lunchroom?' she asked tersely.

'I'd rather wait and let the police allow you to enter,' said the guard.

'How bloody long will they take to get here?' she said, the anger beginning to rise.

'They are on their way, Ma'am,' replied the guard calmly. 'They said they would be here as soon as possible.'

'This is just fucking great,' she said, storming off to her car.

Some of her staff followed and stood around her car. From the side door, the guard could hear she was having a bit of a rant. He smiled to himself.

Twenty minutes later, a car arrived and two people stepped out. They approached the security guard standing by the door.

'Good morning, I'm Cpl Jake North and this Det. Anhton Roberts,' Jake said.

'You're not the police?' said the guard.

'No, I'm DFIS and Det. Roberts is Police liaison with DFIS,' said Jake.

'Who's DFIS?'

'Defence Force Investigative Service,' explained Jake.

Jake turned his head suddenly. Anhton's gaze followed.

'What's going on over there?' asked Jake, indicating the very animated conversation at the car across the carpark.

'That would be the general manger not being allowed inside until it's been cleared,' said the guard.

'She's going to be one to watch,' said Anhton.

Jake turned his attention back to the guard.

'How come you've been sent?' said the guard.

'The call came through to the police, but due to some alerts I've placed, it was transferred to us,' said Jake. 'I believe you've reported a theft at these premises?'

'I did,' replied the guard, a little confused, 'On behalf of Redberg Electronics. Well I believe there has been a theft.'

'What happened?' asked Anhton.

'I guess I can start,' said the guard. 'I arrived at seven am for the shift change over with Garthen Todorovich.'

'Who is he?'

'A fellow guard at Fiyar Security.'

Anhton nodded.

'When I arrived, the side door was unlocked, which is unusual.'

'How so?'

'Well, we mostly stay inside overnight and only come outside for a smoke and to do a walk around of the building.'

'Could he have walked away?'

The guard shook his head. 'No, I don't think so.'

'Were there any problems at home?'

'He isn't married.'

Anhton nodded.

'What happened after you arrived then?' asked Jake.

'I checked the outside of the building, then checked inside. I was careful not to touch anything, but I couldn't find Garthen anywhere. I checked with base and they said they called when they noticed the system go down here at Redberg. Garthen replied that there had been a power failure and that he was waiting for the system to restart. It was out for about thirty minutes, base said.'

'Would they have a log of that conversation?' asked Anhton.

'Yes they will,' said the guard.

'Depending on the investigation, we may need a copy of that.'

The guard nodded.

'What did you do next?' asked Jake.

'By the time I'd finished with base, the first of the employees arrived. I had them check inside, very careful so as not to touch anything and they said that there were some containers of access cards missing.'

'Thank you,' said Anhton. 'Which one of you noticed the missing containers?' Anhton added turning to the other people standing in the group with the guard.

'I did,' said Matt. 'Matt Nuttall, chief technician here at Redberg.'

'What do you know of what's happened today?'

'It only started when I arrived just after seven-thirty this morning,' said Matt. 'We were greeted by the security guard who had informed us of the door being left open and the night guard missing. Then he asked us to carefully check the premises. After an hour, as I was checking the locked cabinet in our office, I noticed that a few containers were missing.'

'Can you show me where this locker is?' asked Anhton.

'Sure, this way,' said Matt. He turned and went to enter the building.

Just as Anhton was about to enter, he heard a shrill voice call from across the carpark. Anhton turned to see what the commotion was and as Jake was closer, he intercepted the advancing group.

'Excuse me,' said the loud, strong female. 'Are you in charge here?'

'I'm Cpl Jake North, DFIS,' said Jake. 'How can I help you?'

'What the fucking hell is going on here?' she demanded. 'I can't afford to stand around here all day while you try and sort out what's happened!'

'I see.' Jake turned to the guard standing by the door. 'Is there somewhere inside these people could wait to be seen by us?'

'They have a lunchroom, which isn't near the office where the lockers are located,' said the guard.

Jake nodded once.

Everyone turned when they heard more vehicles arrive.

'Excellent,' said Jake.

He watched as Gabby, Amy and Dustin walk in his direction.

'I was here first,' demanded the female. She made to push past Jake.

'Don't let anyone enter the building without my express permission. Understood?' snapped Jake to the guard.

'Yes, sir,' replied the guard, smiling. He took up position by the open door, crossed his arms and looked directly at the director of Redberg.

'Glad you guys could make it,' said Jake. 'Night guard missing. Items allegedly missing from a locked cabinet inside. Anhton was about to follow one of the techs to have a look. Gabby, Amy can you check that out?'

'Sure thing.' Gabby and Amy followed Matt inside.

'Anhton, Dustin, you're with me. We need to interview these people, get prints and find out their movements last night,' said Jake. 'Firstly, I want to have a look at these lockers for myself.'

'Sounds like a plan,' said Anhton. 'We'll get the people into the lunchroom and begin chatting to them.'

Jake turned and followed Matt, Gabby and Amy to the office, whilst Anhton and Dustin escorted the general manager and her staff to the lunchroom. Once they were settled, Anhton stood by the only door.

'Here's what I'd like to happen today,' began Anhton. 'Firstly, I'd like each of you to get some paper and a pen.'

One staff member rummaged around in some of the drawers, whilst another went through his bag and soon they had enough paper and pens for everyone.

'Now, I'd like you all to list the following; name, age, contact details, position at the company, and what you did between four pm yesterday and eight am today. I'd also like you to note down anything strange that may have happened over the past day or two. By strange I mean unusual requests for product or information, people hanging around entrances, carparks or nearby streets or shops with intent on viewing these premises. Also, I'd like any information you may happen to have or know about the guard who does the night shift. Once you have done that, hand them over to 2ndLt Coles here and he will collate them for the investigation.'

Once inside the office, Jake visually inspected the locker and was shown the space where the containers would have been.

'What's in the containers?'

'I need to double check the inventory, but I know we'd used some of the blue containers to store the new Forden AV access cards and codes. Even more specific, I think the ones we put away last night were to be used for the new fleets of government, military and diplomatic Fordens.'

'I'll get you to check them once Gabby and Amy have finished,' said Jake.

'Cpl North, I noticed one odd thing,' said Matt.

'What is that?'

'I'm surprised you didn't see them,' he said. He walked out of the room and back to the side door. He stepped outside and walked around the door to the outside. 'These aren't ours.'

Jake saw what Matt was pointing at. A series of three small miniature magnetic road signs stuck to the door. Under one magnet was a seven of clubs playing card.

'Forensics will get it sorted.' Jake pressed a button on his earpiece. 'My sweetest Gabby, are you there?'

'Where do you want me?' came her reply.

'I have some magnets and a playing card attached to the outside of the back door. Would you be so kind as to wield your exceptional talents on the door and the items attached thereon?'

'This will cost you dinner, young man.'

'How does fish and chips on the beach sound?' said Jake.

'Gritty,' said Gabby. 'I'll be right there.'

Jake left the security guard at the side door and went inside to the lunchroom. 'Thank you for waiting, folks,' he said. 'This is what we're going to do. Firstly, I need someone to put a sign on your front door saying you are closed until further notice.' One of the staff members rose and walked towards the door.

'That's not going to happen,' stated the general manager, rising from her seat. 'No one leaves this room to put a sign on the door.'

'As I just said, this office is closed until further notice.' Jake nodded towards the staff member to continue. She did and left the lunchroom.

'Like hell it is,' spat the general manager, striding over and standing in front of Jake.

Jake calmly took a step back and looked at the woman. In her mid-fifties, lean, taller than Jake, her hair tied back tightly, her hazel eyes almost glowing red in anger. 'One more outburst like that and you will be charged with obstruction and taken to a DFIS holding cell. Do you understand?'

'No one orders my business to close.'

'Do you understand?'

The general manager made towards the door, but Jake stepped in front of the exit.

'Get ... Out ... Of ... My ... Way.'

'I will ask again; do you understand?'

The general manager made another step towards the door.

'Fair enough. Anhton, call for another car please?'

'Yes, sir.' He retrieved his phone and dialled the Metro North police station requesting a car to be dispatched to their location.

Jake removed his handcuffs from the back of his pants. 'You are hereby under arrest for obstruction of justice. You will be taken to the Metro North police station where you will wait.' He placed the first cuff onto her wrist, turned her around and secured the second.

'You can't do this to me!'

Jake pulled a chair to a corner of the room, gently sat the general manger down and had Anhton watch her.

'Dustin, we need fingerprints of everyone in this room so that we can check them against any prints found on the side door and from the cabinet in the locker room,' said Jake.

'I can do that for you,' said Dustin.

After five minutes of the general manager ranting and raving, Jake had had enough.

'Anhton, can you take her to our car and sit her in that, windows closed until the other car arrives?'

'Yes, Sir.' Anhton assisted the general manager to her feet and escorted her outside to the car.

Anhton returned to the lunchroom once the second car had taken the general manager back to the station.

It took about ninety minutes for the forensics team to scour the building. Once they packed up and left, Jake returned to the lunchroom, where the staff were now quite anxious.

As Jake walked in, he was assaulted with all sorts of questions. Some in anger over the treatment of their general manager. Some asking if they could get back to work. Others wanting to know what was going on. Jake called for calm.

'Firstly, I sincerely apologise for the way I handled your general manager, but I did what I felt was necessary at the time to keep order,' said Jake. 'Secondly, you are permitted to go back to work. If your area is covered in dust, it is okay to clean it away now. The forensics team have all the data they need.' He turned to Matt. 'Matt, I'd like you and your colleagues to check the inventory and let me know what access cards are missing. The sooner I know, the better it will help my investigation.'

'We'll let you know as soon as we can Cpl,' replied Matt.

'Thank you. We'll be off now. If we have any further questions, we will let you know,' said Jake. 'Anhton, do you have everyone's statements?'

'Yes I do, except for the general manager,' he said.

'Ah yes. We had better go and have a talk to her,' said Jake. 'Good day to you all,' he added and they left the building.

Anhton waited until they were safely in the car before he spoke. 'Did you have to treat the general manager that way?'

'I did what I thought was needed,' replied Jake calmly. 'At the time, you seemed to be pleased.'

'Don't get me wrong, I think she was being rather bitchy, but I'm sure you could've handled it differently.'

Jake smiled. 'Perhaps and no doubt she will have something to say to me when I get to the station.'

'Ya think?' said Anhton. 'Can you make 'Obstruction' stick if she complains?'

'Do you agree with my call on that?'

'Sure.'

'Then I can make it stick,' said Jake. 'I'll tell the boss before I go speak to her.'

* * * * *

Jake put his satchel on his desk the following morning and opened his email. He read the forensics report. As he was finishing, Anhton arrived at his desk, next to Jake's.

'What are you reading, boss?' he asked.

'The forensics report from yesterday.'

'Do we know anything new?'

'Not really. All the fingerprints found belong to the staff or the missing security guard. The magnetic road signs found on the door can be purchased from any gift shop around town. The playing card is also standard stock. It could come from any deck anywhere.'

'How are we going to sort this one out? Was it an inside job then?'

'We won't know that until we can verify the whereabouts of all the staff concerned. We also need to find the missing guard, Garthen Todorovic.'

'Jake, isn't the playing card like the one we found several weeks ago at the explosives leads factory?'

'I don't know. Let me have a look.'

Jake pressed a few keys and soon they were looking at the file from forensics for the *Blasted Leads* case. He flipped through the report to get to the pictures attached. When the pictures popped up, they looked at images of both sides of the card.

'It's a different number and suit, of course, but looks the same to me,' said Anhton. 'Did forensics check the card?'

'Let's see,' said Jake. He flipped back over the notes. 'It doesn't look like it. We'd better get them to double check.' Jake tapped away at his keyboard and sent an email to forensics to check the card. 'Hopefully that will bring up a result.'

An alarm sounded on Jake's computer screen.

'Ah, an email from Matt Nuttall, at Redberg Electronics.' Jake opened and read the email.

'What does he say?'

'This is interesting.'

'What is?' said Anhton.

'The access codes for the Forden AVs that were stolen? They are for the fleets of new government, military and diplomatic vehicles, as Matt surmised yesterday. This is getting more intriguing.'

4.3

Jake switched on the TV as he dried himself off after his shower. Waiting for the kettle to finish boiling, he sat down to watch the morning variety program. His interest was piqued by the text flashing across the bottom of the screen;

'Police and DFIS colluding in hiding the truth from the public.'

Jake turned up the volume. The hosts of the morning program had crossed to a reporter standing outside his nearest police station.

'This is Derik Scott and I'm here to report that the Police and DFIS are colluding to hide the truth from the public. Since January, and including an incident yesterday, four men are missing, presumed dead. Also, a quantity of D6 has been stolen from the military. A couple of months later, blasting caps, then some slapper leads and then a number of access cards and codes were stolen from Redberg Electrics.'

'Shit.' Jake got up and turned off the screaming kettle and sat back down again.

'Furthermore, of the four men that are missing, I know three of them personally. Many years ago, I served in an army unit on deployment overseas. One missing man was my former CO, Vic Forde, another was a comrade Damian Smithson and only yesterday, I have now discovered, another comrade, Garthen Todorovic is missing. Whilst it's too early to speculate over Garthen, I know for a fact that Damian and Vic have not been heard from since they disappeared. I can only presume they are now dead and nothing is being done about it.'

'Crap, crap, crap, crap, crap!'

Jake jumped up, his towel falling to the floor, as he answered his phone vibrating excitedly on the bench.

'North here, how can I help? ... Morning, Linda ... yes, I do happen to be watching what's on TV right now ... no, I have not said anything to anyone at the media ... I will investigate as to how this was leaked ... yes, I'll be there as soon as I can.'

Thirty minutes later, Jake pulled into his parking spot and raced to his desk. Grabbing his tablet, he began to flip through the data as he walked to the Glass room. Pressing a button on the corner of the table, he waited impatiently for the few seconds whilst the Glass activated. He entered his access code and waited again.

'Morning, Jake,' said the human computerised voice.

'Morning, Lassie. I have some data for you.'

'Which file, Jake?'

'Dee-eff-eye-ess-zero-four-zero-one-jay-enn.'

'Accessing.'

Jake stopped reading and prepared the tablet for upload.

'Available for upload.'

'Acknowledged, Lassie. Uploading now.'

Jake watched the upload bar move across the bottom of the large glass table in front of him.

'Received and compiling now.'

'Transfer to vertical.' Vertical was the name given to the latest upgrade of the Glass they were using allowing data to be transferred from the glass top to a floating 'screen'.

'Acknowledged,' said Lassie.

Jake looked up and saw the new information popping up on the screen. He put his tablet to one side and began to move the data around.

'Now to add the details of the news report from this morning.' As Jake processed the data, a red box appeared around the name of Derik Scott. *This is too much to be a coincidence. Why is everyone involved attached to this army unit? Is there something they are not telling me?*

Anhton walked in to the Glass to see Jake deep in thought.

'What ya got for me, sexy?' said Anhton.

'Not what you want,' replied Jake without turning around. 'Did you see the morning news today?'

'No, why?'

'Have a look at this.' Jake pressed play on the recording he had of the news report by Derik.

'That's puts a spanner in the works,' said Anhton.

'It does somewhat?' I've loaded all the data from yesterday and Lassie is still compiling, but even before that's finished, I already have a red box around Derik's name. He is another member of the army unit.'

'Are we sure they weren't covert ops? What if this Derik is behind it all? How else would he know that so many people are missing from his old unit, these things haven't been released to the public yet.'

'I know,' said Jake. 'We'll need to keep a very close eye on him now.'

Jake sat in silence for several minutes.

'I need to speak to Linda,' he said. 'Can you look after this for the moment?'

'Sure,' said Anhton.

Jake walked along the hall until he got to Linda's office. He saw that David was already inside talking with her, so he turned and walked away.

'Come in, Jake, Linda wants a word with you,' called David from the office door.

Jake walked in and sat down opposite her desk.

'Talk to me.' said Linda.

'Please forgive me, I'm about to give a reduced version of my current stream of consciousness as I haven't had a chance to process it,' said Jake.

'I understand,' said Linda.

'So, Derik Scott, a member of the same unit as yourself and Vic and Damian ...'

'...Yes, as well as Danika Wordsworth, Peter Dugald, Vienata Grond-Fiala, and Giulia Quinn,' interjected Linda.

Jake nodded. 'How is it that Derik has all this information about Vic and Damian? Nothing has been released to the public. What did Derik do as part of the unit? Were you covert ops? Or trained?'

'We weren't covert ops, nor were we trained as such,' said Linda. 'However, Derik was always one to ask questions. He would ask who we were, where we came from, family, why we joined the army, and so on. We all got sick of it and told him on many occasions, but when things were silent between us all, he would chirp up again. I have a feeling he didn't like silence, nor did he seem to not like not knowing.'

'I have an uneasy feeling about Derik, Ma'am,' said Jake.

'How so, Jake?' said Linda.

'I can't pinpoint it. Perhaps it's just the fact that he knows this information without it having been told to anyone.'

'Do you have any news on Garthen?' asked Linda.

'Not at this stage. He is listed with us as missing, and we are presuming dead, along with Vic and Damian. I'm sorry, Linda.'

'Don't be,' she said. 'We were good together but I doubt any of us would've made life-long friends anyway. Don't get me wrong, we'd never be enemies either.'

'I understand,' said Jake. 'I'm still stuck for a motive, if indeed these incidents are related. The obvious shouts at me though.'

'Do tell?' asked Linda.

'A bomb for starters. D6, followed by caps and then leads,' said Jake. 'I'm not sure how the stolen access cards fit in though.'

'In the meantime?' said Linda.

'I'm going over all the data we have so far to see if there's anything I've missed,' said Jake.

'Very well, don't let me keep you.'

Jake left the office, whilst David stayed.

'Something on your mind, David?'

'I think we should call the remaining members of the army unit in for a meeting.'

'What will that achieve?'

'An awareness to be a little more vigilant. Three of you have gone missing in a matter of months. Nothing may happen, of course, but I think it wise the others be made aware that these three buddies have disappeared under unusual circumstances, with no word.'

'Agreed. Make it happen and let me know when it is. I'm happy to address them myself.'

'Yes, Ma'am.' David left the office.

* * * * *

Two days later, Jake walked into the office. He passed a number of nervous looking people in the foyer. He made his way to his desk and dropped his satchel. He removed his tablet, accessed a file and went to the Glass.

'Morning, Lassie,' he said, once the screen was activated.

'Good morning, Jake,' Lassie replied.

'Has everyone arrived for the meeting today?'

'Let me check ... Jeremy Pyke is the only one who hasn't checked in yet. ... Wait, he's just signed in. Everyone's here now, Jake.'

'Thank you, Lassie.'

Jake left the Glass zone and saw Linda at her desk. 'Are you ready for the meeting?'

'As ready as I'll ever be.'

'Would you like to collect them?'

'Sure. What room are we in?'

'Conference Two, Level One,' said David, crossing the room from his office.

Linda nodded. 'I'll go and get my army buddies and see you in the conference room soon.'

'Have we got everyone here, Jake?' asked David.

'Yes, Lassie just confirmed the last one checked in moments ago.'

'Let's get to the conference room. We'll make this meeting as short as possible.'

'Very good.'

David and Jake left the office, rode the elevator to Level One and waited in Conference Room Two for their guests to arrive. Linda soon arrived and showed the six guests into the room.

Jake and David greeted them in turn.

Jake could understand why Danika was popular in the presidential vote. She was confident, but not showing any arrogance. She dressed smartly in matching light-grey jacket and pants and a neatly fitting pale-lemon shirt but was comfortable. Whilst her face was clear, it showed no specific emotion or reaction for being at DFIS HQ. However, Jake noticed in her eyes that she was a little nervous as she carefully regarded each of her former colleagues.

Cmdr Peter Dugald walked in holding Danika's hand. He wore his Army dress uniform and responded accordingly to the various greetings and salutes. Peter was tanned, fit, but not lean. His face was militarily strict yet emanated a warmth that belied his outward persona. Jake remembered Peter warmly from his own time at Williams Defence Force Base. Jake was surprised when he noticed how much his eyes would land on Danika. *Was there more than it seemed?*, thought Jake.

Jake regarded Derik Scott a little longer than Danika and Peter. Here was the man that had made the report the morning before on live television. Derik was a short, solidly built man, but not one to get angry with. Well, perhaps when he was younger. For now, he was a threat in a different way. Wearing jeans, a blue check shirt, over a white skivvy and a dark jacket, Derik sat confidently, removed a pad and pen and waited. A smug looked crossed his face when he saw Jake looking at him.

Vienata Grond-Fiala sat opposite Danika. Vienata wore an older style kilt-skirt, a white shirt and a green jacket. She greeted everyone warmly and sat comfortably. Whilst her eyes looked from person to person, she did not appear nervous. She came across as quite relaxed.

After shaking hands with Jake, Jeremy Pyke slumped into a seat at the end of the table. He was smartly dressed in jeans, collared shirt and a zip jacket. He certainly wasn't dishevelled as his actions intimated. He calmly looked around at those in the room and finally he caught Jake's gaze. At that he straightened up, pulled himself up to the table and returned the gaze. Jake didn't flinch and calmly took his seat at the opposite end of the table.

Finally, there was Giulia Quinn. She was the most nervous of all. She sat on the other side of Danika and kept her eyes on the President-elect. She wore a long coat over her navy-blue dress with an almost matronly pair of navy-blue court shoes. Whilst she may have been quite svelte in the army, as it still showed, she looked a little less fit now.

'Good morning, folks. Have a seat,' said David, as they all took seats. 'I'm 2ndLt David Castle. This is my colleague Crpl Jake North.'

They acknowledged the introductions.

'You're probably wondering why you've been called here today,' said David.

Most nodded, others just looked at David, or each other.

'Why are we here? I can see that you have gathered the army unit together. What's going on?' Derik Scott, Channel 8,' said Derik.

'As you now know,' David continued, pointedly ignoring the interruption, 'Damian Smithson was reported missing earlier this year, followed by Vic Forde and now Garthen Todorovic appears to be missing. All because of robberies at the premises at which they worked. We had our reasons to keep things quiet. Not every investigation needs to be reported.'

'The people had the right to know. You cannot withhold information like this from the public,' fumed Derik. 'I still don't understand what this has to do with us?'

'Speaking of which,' said David, 'How did you come to know?'

Derik immediately went tight-lipped.

David nodded his head.

'Regarding your question, hopefully nothing at all,' said David. 'All we want you to do is be careful.'

'How do you mean, 2ndLt?' asked Danika. Tall for a female, at 183cm, with lightly tanned skin, and all natural dark blonde hair. She wore little make-up but didn't need to. Her dark green eyes stood out and often people found themselves being drawn into whatever it was she was speaking about at the time. Never one to solely rely on her looks, Danika was also very smart and well educated.

'President-elect Wordsworth. Congratulations, by the way.'

'Thank you 2ndLt,' said Danika.

'Please, you can call me, David. What I mean by being careful is that your former army colleagues have disappeared under unusual circumstances and we still have no knowledge of where they are. We think there is a connection between their disappearances, but we need proof. We would rather not have to investigate another disappearance of someone from your former army unit.'

'Surely that's just coincidence?' asked Peter. 'I still have two soldiers missing from January. Cullen wasn't part of this unit.'

'No he wasn't, Peter, but he is military,' said David. 'Of the four incidents we've been involved in, only one hasn't resulted in a disappearance. The others have had current or ex-service military personnel involved. We don't think it's a coincidence.'

'What are we supposed to do then?' asked Derik. 'Walk around paranoid? Why haven't you or the police been able to do anything to catch the person involved?'

'The investigation is ongoing,' said David.

'Can you vouch for this, Linda?' asked Derik.

'Absolutely I can, Derik,' said Linda. 'I'd like to ask that if any of you, knows anything, we need to let the team here at DFIS know. You can contact me, if that's more comfortable for you, and I will make sure it is investigated. I have faith in my colleagues that we will come to a conclusion.'

'No one here will be any help.' said Jeremy. 'As usual, they are incompetent and don't know a thing.'

'That's enough, Jeremy,' said Linda, sternly. 'I am personally keeping an eye on proceedings. These things take time. Eventually, the person behind this will make a mistake and we'll be there to catch them.'

'No you won't,' said Jeremy, quietly. Those close by heard him. Jake also heard him and looked at him sharply.

'Thank you, Linda,' said David. 'We are working as hard as we can with the information provided to obtain a quick resolution.'

'Sounds like military spin to me,' said Derik. 'Why haven't we heard of this in the news before this? People need to know that robberies and disappearances are happening.'

'No thanks to you Derik,' said David.

'David!' said Linda.

'It is being kept out of the news purposely to ensure we have a clean investigation,' said David.

'The people need to know,' said Derik.

'There will be no more information released to the public,' David said firmly. 'Is that understood by all?' The last part was delivered directly to Derik.

Derik moved forward in his seat, but Linda placed her hand on his forearm and he sat back.

'Is that understood?'

Everyone nodded, even Derik who responded begrudgingly.

'Unless you have any pressing questions, I will thank you for your time and Linda will show you out.'

* * * * *

Jake sat in the Glass zone typing away at the keyboard displayed on the Glass table. A few moments later, David joined him.

'What do you think, Jake?'

'About?'

'The army unit?'

'I watched each of them and made some notes on their reactions. I'm uploading my notes now.'

David watched as the files loaded and he read Jake's comments as they appeared under each of the photos of the remaining unit members.

Danika Wordsworth: President-elect, quiet, unassuming, thoughtful, she listened to all that was being said and only spoke when it was necessary and was clear and concise,

Jeremy Pyke: reserved, cold-ish, his eyes darted all over the place, he generally seemed nervous about something, not sure if he's hiding something or not,

Peter Dugald: still serving in the military as CO at Williams Defence Force Base, seems to be in a relationship with Danika, but that seems to be kept quiet still, not sure why that would be,

Derik Scott: reporter, brash, unrelenting, ready to blame anyone he can, seems to have a distaste for both the police and the military, will step on toes and won't seem to care, one to watch,

Vienata Grond-Fiala: a rather grond name for someone so diminutive, whilst quiet throughout the meeting, I think she would be someone who was feisty,

Giulia Quinn: seemed timid to me, sat next to Danika and always looked to her when something was being said, what is her relationship to Danika?, it would seem it's more of a protective thing, than earned.

'Interesting observations there, Jake,' said David.

'Thank you. I took the opportunity to sit back and watch.'

'Should we be watching any of them?'

'You think it's one of their own?'

'I don't think anything, but all avenues have to be kept open.'

Jake stroked his chin. 'At this stage, I doubt any of them are involved.'

'Okay.'

'Without seeing more detailed psych profiles, they may well have been reacting as they react to any sort of information being given to them.'

4.4

Giulia Quinn took her phone from her bag in a desk drawer as soon as Danika's meeting began. She flipped through until she found the number she wanted.

'Calderwood Industries, how may I direct your call?'

'I'd like to speak to Ms. M please.'

'One moment.'

Giulia heard the familiar series of clicks and white noise before Ms. M answered.

'Giulia, we don't hear from you that often. What's the problem?'

'Three of my former army colleagues are dead, technically missing, but I'm sure they're dead,' Giulia said firmly. 'What if I'm next?'

'Calm down, we're keeping our eye on you. You're safe. Just do what you've been told to do and we'll take care of the rest.'

'I don't know ...'

'Stay focussed and you'll be fine.'

The call was terminated and Giulia went back to her work.

Ms. M sat at her desk and simply stared ahead. It was a few minutes before a knock at the door brought her out of her trance..

'Come in.'

The man who entered was in his 60s, silver hair, green eyes and walked with an almost imperceptible limp. He wore black jeans, rolled at the ankle, a white shirt and an auburn-coloured waistcoat. He also wore ankle high dark red leather laced boots. He crossed the room confidently and quietly.

'Are you okay, Bryony?' asked the man.

'What? Yes, I am,' she said. 'Sir.' She stood.

'I'm not the president, you don't have to stand when I walk into a room.' He sat down on the other side of her desk.

'I think we need to review our recruiting processes,' said Bryony.

'Why do you say that?'

'Our operative in the president-elect's office is getting jittery.'

'What about?' asked the man.

'Her former army unit has recently lost some members and she doesn't want to be next.'

'What did you say to her?'

'To do her job and that we're keeping our eye on her,' said Bryony.

'Perhaps we should check on her concerns?'

'I can look into it.'

The man stood. 'Let me know what you find.'

He left Bryony's office.

4.5

Jake finished adding his thoughts to the Glass after the meeting with the ex-army unit was finished. Afterward, Jake left the office early, spent a couple of hours at the gym and went home.

After enjoying a light meal, he prepared his spot in the middle of the lounge room floor. His newest meditation music playing and his essential oils burning, he practiced his daily routine of reflection and meditation. He went through a series of yoga moves and finally settled on his mat in a seated position.

- Another ex-army man, working for a security company, disappeared, presumed dead, but no proof.

- Access cards and codes stolen for the newest Forden AVs, in particular for the new fleets of government, military and diplomatic vehicles.

- Alerts to be expanded further to check for thefts of Forden AVs.

- Three of the four missing men belonged to the same army unit ten years previously.

- A meeting was called of the remaining unit members, who were alerted to keep vigilance, especially when alone.

- Not all the unit members convinced the circumstances surrounding the missing men are related.

- Must keep an eye on Derik Scott, he could be a loose cannon.

- Do the stolen D6, blasting caps and leads, access cards and codes, and the missing ex-army unit men have anything in common at all?

- One serving military personnel still missing.

- LCmdr Linda Barrow getting very antsy about the delays.

Jake sat for another hour before stretching and going for a jog before bed.

As he jogged, he had the distinct impression he was being followed. Each time he turned there was no one there. At one stage he was certain he caught a glimpse of a shadow ducking behind a tree.

He sped up his jog and as soon as he turned a corner, where he knew there was cover, he quickly hid behind the driveway pillar of one of the properties.

Slowing his breathing as quickly as possible, he waited quietly. He heard steps turn the corner and stop. Slowly they moved towards him.

At that moment, a light flicked on at the front of the house that owned the pillar he was hiding behind. The approaching footsteps stopped. Jake was still hidden in the dark shadow of the pillar.

Jake then he heard the footsteps move away and speed up. He came out of his hiding place and headed back along the path to the corner of the street. No one was in sight.

Jake took a little longer than normal to jog home, making sure he took streets that would lead away from his home. When he felt it safe, he turned and headed for home.

Keeping the house dark for half an hour after getting home, he monitored his street. There was no further suspicious behaviour, so he went to bed.

Unfortunately, he didn't sleep well at all that night.

4.6

Jeremy Pyke drove to Dawn Forde's home after he had left the meeting at the DFIS offices. He knew that she had a day off and was hoping to further their burgeoning relation- ship He pulled into the driveway to find her digging in the front garden.

'Morning, beautiful,' greeted Jeremy, as he got out of his car.

'Morning, Jeremy,' said Dawn, leaning her shovel against a tree. 'What brings you here?'

'I was called to a meeting at DFIS HQ this morning.'

'DFIS, what did they want?'

'The rest of the old army unit was there.'

'Oh.' Tears welled up in her eyes.

Jeremy stepped forward and hugged her.

'I don't know what I would've done without you being here, Jeremy. I can't thank you enough.'

'Hey, Dawn, I'm always here for you, no matter what. I know how much Vic loved you and for him to be missing is still not right.'

They hugged a little more.

'What say you go get yourself cleaned up and I'll take you somewhere nice for lunch?'

'I'd like that,' said Dawn.

'Great.'

Jeremy waited in the lounge room for Dawn to get ready. As he did, he looked around the room. His gaze lingered for quite some time on the array of photos that hung on one wall. Photos of the army unit. Of Jeremy and Vic together. Of Jeremy, Vic and dawn and the kids on a holiday on the river. One Jeremy knew he couldn't stay long for. He stood and gently stroked Dawn in the picture.

Jeremy realised that Vic had looked after her and the boys well. The furniture was new, albeit a few years old. Throw rugs and cushions were everywhere. The latest in TVs sat on a low table opposite the couch. The curtains were fresh, clean and of a dark grey. This was offset by the light grey feature wall behind the TV with the rest of the walls a cream colour.

It had been a few years since Jeremy had been to the house and knew that Vic would have done the renovations with Dawn helping and giving instruction as to what she wanted.

Dawn reappeared wearing a pair of blue jeans, a long-sleeved shirt, a thick woollen jumper and a long coat was over her arm.

'You do look good, Dawn,' said Jeremy as he escorted her to the car.

'So do you. Very smart indeed,' said Dawn.

Jeremy wore a pair of black jeans, a light-yellow shirt and a black jumper.

'Where are we going today?' asked Dawn.

'I thought we'd go to Brighton. Look out over the bay. Watch the ships go by, and by the looks of it, the storm roll in.'

After lunch, they came back to Dawn's place.

'When do the boys get home?' asked Jeremy.

'They have sport after school,' said Dawn. 'I don't need to collect them until about six.'

'We have some time then?' Jeremy said, as they hugged on her doorstep.

'We do, but...'

'What is it, Dawn?' Jeremy hugged her tighter.

'I still feel unfaithful to Vic. He may still be alive.'

'I understand that and if he does come back, I will walk away. If he doesn't come back, you have me.'

Dawn placed her head on Jeremy's chest, closed her eyes and rested for a moment. Jeremy looked over her head and smiled.

'Let's enjoy the time we have,' said Jeremy. 'You do enjoy our time together, don't you?'

'Of course I do,' said Dawn. She let go of his embrace, opened the door, took him by the hand and led him inside.

A couple of hours later, as Jeremy and Dawn lay snuggling in her bed, her mobile phone rang. She reached over to answer it.

Jeremy reached around her waist when she sat upright.

'Madam Wordsworth, how can I help you? ... I know you're my aunt, but I never know what to say when you call ... ok, Danika. How can I help you? ... Oh, are you sure ... yes, I accept. Do you need me to come and sign some paperwork?

... Yes, I can come and see you at your office tomorrow. When will this appointment begin? ... That soon ... yes Madame President. Thank you very much.'

Dawn put the phone back on the bedside table.

'What was all that about?' asked Jeremy.

'President-elect Wordsworth has asked me to be her Chief of Security.'

'That's fantastic, Dawn.' Jeremy kissed her. 'When do you start?'

'Monday week.'

'So soon?'

'Yeah. She wants me on board so that I can get a good team together for independence and inauguration in November.'

'How will your boss take the news?'

'Like all good bosses. Not well.'

'It will work to your advantage anyway. Doesn't the new President want a full integration of military and domestic police?'

'She does and I know that has begun, but I guess part of my role might be to see that it happens by November 18.'

'Congratulations, babe, this is fantastic for you.'

'Thank you, Jeremy.'

'Dawn?'

'Yes, what is it?'

'I love you.'

'Oh,' said Dawn.

'What's the matter?'

'I want to love you, but what if Vic comes back?'

'Let yourself have some enjoyment and love. Like I said, if Vic returns, I will walk away and leave you be.'

'I don't know.'

'Think of the boys. What would Vic want you to do for them?'

Dawn rolled over and allowed Jeremy to hold her close to him.

'The boys do really like you,' she said.

'I love the boys too and I will treat them as if they were my own. It's the least I can do for Vic.'

'This is so hard, but I do love you Jeremy,' said Dawn, rolling over to face him again. They kissed passionately and made love again.

4.7

David walked into the office the following morning to find Linda pacing back and forth. She strode right up to David when she saw him.

'Did you see the news last night?' she said strongly.

'Yes I did, Ma'am,' said David.

'I know for a fact that you told him not to say a word.'

'Yes I did.'

'Then how did Derik get to make such an outlandish report,' said Linda, the ire rising in her voice rapidly. 'He made us look like fools and incompetents.'

'I will give him a call and gag him.'

'I've had my boss, the police commissioner and Danika's office down my throat this morning.'

'She should've known that he was gagged, she was here yesterday.'

'I don't care who was here or not, get that story retracted and have that reporter gagged. Threaten him with jail if you have to.'

'Yes, Ma'am.'

Linda began to walk towards her office but paused. 'I want this wrapped up as soon as possible, David.'

'Yes Ma'am.'

4.8

A door opened and closed in the far left corner of the basement of a warehouse in the inner west of Melbourne. Five drums sat bunched on the back of the large, matte-black utility and were covered with a black tarpaulin.

With the silencer fully active on the ute, it drove quietly from the warehouse, its load secure. Without rushing, the ute headed southwest towards Altona and travelled along a road leading to the coast a little further south.

Turning off the sealed road, the ute travelled a short distance, the driver opened and closed a farm gate and smoothly rode the track to a darkened shed. The shed was opened and the ute backed in. Once the door was closed, low lighting was activated and the ute backed up until it was almost touching a large matte-black cruising boat. The drums were rolled onto the boat and secured.

With sophisticated sensor arrays and radar activated, the lights inside the shed were switched off. The doors of the shed were opened and the boat slipped silently from its moorings. Once manoeuvred to a deep part of Port Phillip Bay, the boat stopped. The rear gate of the boat was opened and the drums were released and they rolled into the bay. With weights used as their lids, they sank quickly into the murky depths.

After the last drum had sunk out of view, the rear gate was closed and the boat retuned to the shed. Over the next hour, the boat was thoroughly cleaned and hosed down with salt water. A thickish liquid was poured over the boat so that almost every part of any visible surface was covered.

Cables that had been hung around the walls were then connected to various parts of the boat. These cables led to a small array of batteries to the left of the main doors. Wires were connected to the batteries and the cables. Sitting on a shelf above the batteries, an electronic timer was set to sixty.

The ute was driven out of the shed, stopped whilst the door to the shed was locked and then continued its way back to the warehouse basement it was stored in. From the roof of the warehouse, with a second timer sitting on the ledge, a pair of high-powered binoculars were trained on a spot along the coast.

As the buzzer sounded on the timer, a fireball was seen rising in the distance. Those who lived close by heard an extremely loud explosion, just before the fireball erupted. Even with the lights blaring from the oil refineries on the coast at Altona, the fireball was still visible in the night sky. The timer and binoculars were stowed in a cupboard in the sub-basement.

A door in the far left corner opened and closed.

5.1

For five nights, the new electronics warehouse store in Burwood had been watched. In the chill of the August night,
the only thing giving away the presence of anyone was the
occasional mist of an exhaled breath. The matte-black ute
parked in almost the same spot every night; in front of a rundown house in a side street. Suspicions were aroused when
the owner of the rundown house came out to see the outline
of the darkened ute pull into the spot in front. He walked
up and inspected the ute, but nothing or no one responded.
Every night for the following four nights, he watched and
waited.

For two of those nights, the owner sat on his darkened
porch and watched a figure jog back and forth in the same
direction. During the day, the owner retraced the steps to
the end of the street and could only surmise as to where the

figure went from there. It could've been to the left, or to the right, where the new electronics store was located.

One night, the homeowner decided to do something about the strange visitor.

He waited in the dark near his front driveway. Eventually the figure came jogging back towards the ute. The homeowner walked to the ute and stood by the front, waiting.

He watched the figure slow and stop, still several metres away from the ute. The homeowner began to back away and the figure moved closer. The homeowner walked forward and the figure stopped. Suddenly, the figure moved and approached the ute. Without a word, the driver's door opened.

The homeowner made his move and walked to the open door. He stopped it from closing.

'What's your game, buddy?'

Silence.

'I'll call the police if you don't tell me what you're doing here and why this ute is so dark.'

Silence.

An attempt was made to close the ute's door.

'Oh no, you're not going anywhere. I get what I want,' said the homeowner.

Silence.

Another attempt was made to close the door, but the homeowner held fast.

Suddenly, the homeowner found himself face first on

the bonnet of the ute. His right was arm wrenched behind his back to the point of breaking. The homeowner was a strong man and struggled free. In the ensuing scuffle, the sleeve of the figure was torn, revealing a distinctive tattoo.

The homeowner froze.

'I know you. You're...'

The homeowner was unable to complete his sentence as his neck was snapped quickly to the left. The limp body was dumped in the back of the ute and covered.

'Shit!'

The darkened ute drove away from the street before turning the lights on.

Thirty minutes later, the ute was driving into the basement of a building. The body in the back was placed into a large drum and was liquefied, as those before him.

* * * * *

The following night, the ute parked in the same spot in the same street in front of the same house.

At the electronics store, the last of the staff members was preparing to leave. The back door had been left open and the figure slipped inside. The staff member set the alarm, closed, and locked the door.

Inside, the figure, hidden on top of one the shelving units in the storeroom, pulled a small tablet from its backpack. Silently, the alarm system was deactivated. Moving quickly, the figure located what it wanted, unlocked the rear door and slipped away into the night.

The ute was driven away from the address but parked a short distance away, around a corner. The shadow picked up some items from the front seat. Jogging to the electronics store, a toy model of an Austin Healey and a six of spades playing card were left hanging from the back door. A second playing card was left in the letterbox of the resident who had confronted the shadow. Just as the shadow jogged away, a security company car arrived at the store.

The ute returned to its basement garage. A small item was placed in a locked cupboard on one wall.

A door in the far left corner opened and closed.

5.2

The security guard pulled up to the rear of the electronics store. He walked around the rear yard but saw nothing out of the ordinary. He went to open the back door but hesitated when he saw the toy car and playing card, hanging from the door. He radioed back to base and they agreed to call someone back to the store.

Twenty minutes later, another car pulled into the rear yard of the store.

A thin, wiry man in his thirties stepped from the car.

The guard approached. 'Good evening. Sorry to call you out like this,' said the guard.

'That's okay. The security company said something about the alarm being turned off,' said the thin man.

'Yes, that's why I'm here. I checked the perimeter and things seemed fine. It was when I went to check the back door that I found something odd.'

'Oh? What is it?'

'Come have a look.' The guard led the thin man to the back door. 'Are those yours?'

The thin man looked at the toy car and card. 'Not mine personally, nor do they belong to the store. I was the one to lock up tonight so I can be certain of that. Unless one of the boys is playing a joke.'

'Do you have a tissue or hanky on you?'

'Why do you want to know that?' the thin man looked at the guard oddly.

'Well, if you're going to check the back door, you don't want to leave any prints.'

'I closed the door in the first place and locked it. Why would I want to check it?' said the thin man. 'Besides, extra prints of mine won't make a difference.'

'They will if there are new ones over the top of yours,' said the guard.

The thin man dropped his shoulders, pulled a hanky from his pocket and gingerly checked the door. It opened, causing the thin man to stop.

'I know I locked this door before I left earlier tonight. I double-checked to make sure it was locked. Is the alarm still off too?'

'Yes,' said the guard. 'It hasn't been turned on again.'

'I'm not happy about this, I want to call the police.'

'I think you should.'

The thin man stepped away from the back door, pulled his phone from his pocket and dialled the police. Thirty minutes later, a police car arrived. The guard and the thin man explained everything they knew to the two officers who attended. They then called back to their base and were told that crime scene investigators would attend. Another twenty-minute wait for the detectives to arrive.

After an initial consultation with the uniformed police officers, the two new arrivals approached the back door.

'Good evening, I'm Det.Sgt Amita Brookes and this is my colleague Det. Anhton Roberts,' said Amita. 'We've been briefed by the other officers.'

As Amita talked to the thin man and the guard, Anhton was looking at the door with the toy and card hanging from the handle.

'Det.Sgt, can I have a word please?' asked Anhton.

'What is it Roberts?' asked Amita.

'You know how I've been on secondment with DFIS for the past few months?'

'Painfully so.'

'I don't think it'll be worth our while investigating any further,' said Anhton. 'As part of the ongoing investigations, this card here almost matches exactly to those cases that have had similar cards left behind.'

'What do you suggest then, Roberts?'

'We hand over to DFIS, Ma'am. They investigated the first instance of the card, and it seems they've become involved with every other instance since. Might as well get them here right now. Might save time and will allow the trail to be a whole lot warmer.'

'I'm sure we can handle this, Roberts.'

'They'll be asked to get involved anyway, and we're integrating after all.'

'You're all for the integration, aren't you?'

'Yes, Ma'am. Best decision ever made, in my book.'

'Very well, call them. You can stay here and I want you to keep me updated at all times,' said Amita.

'Yes, Ma'am. Thank you, Ma'am.'

Amita left and drove back to base with one of the other police officers. The remaining one was given instruction to return Anhton to base when he was finished. Anhton called DFIS and was put through to David's mobile at home. After explaining the situation to David, he agreed to come as soon as he could.

About midnight, David arrived with Jake.

They got out of the car and walked to where three men were huddled.

'Hey Anhton, what you got?'

'Hey, David,' said Anhton. 'This is Bud Haliwell, manager of the electronics store.'

'Good evening, Mr Haliwell,' said David.

'Can we make this quick, please?' asked Bud. 'It's late and it's cold.'

'We'll do our best.' David nodded at Jake, who began to check the door. 'Do you know if anything's been taken?'

'How can I, I haven't been allowed inside.'

Anhton moved beside Jake and smiled. 'Hey, sexy,' he whispered.

Jake smirked, blushed and blew Anhton a kiss.

Everyone turned when a van rolled into the rear car park.

'You'll be able to get inside soon, Mr Haliwell. Our forensics team have arrived,' said David. 'Anhton, is there anything out of the ordinary?'

'This toy car and card, sir,' Anhton replied.

'I have them, David,' called Jake. 'Dusted and bagged.'

Yawning, Amy and Gabby approached. Gabby held a strong smelling coffee.

'Get your kit and get working. Have Gabby give you a hand. Amy, stay with me,' ordered David.

Jake retrieved his kit from the car and began working on the items. Gabby began dusting the rest of the door.

'Oh, Gabby' added David. 'We have another card and item to check. Make sure you get good pics of their location. I want these so thoroughly checked that there's no possible way a print can't be missed.'

'Got it,' said Gabby.

'Shall we go inside?' said David.

David put on a rubber glove and carefully opened the door, whilst Gabby dusted it for prints. She'd already photo-graphed, tagged and bagged the toy car and card.

'Okay, Mr Haliwell, follow us and let us know if any-thing has been disturbed, but don't touch.'

Bud nodded his head.

David stopped at the security panel inside the door and traced it to the switchboard. He stepped outside and soon Amy joined him. 'Amy, I want this panel and the switchboard over there dusted.'

'Yes, sir,' replied Amy.

David, Anhton and Bud moved carefully along the aisles of stock in the storeroom. As they travelled down an aisle close to the rear wall of the store itself, Bud stopped.

He leant in to look at an open box but moved away to the next bay. This time he stopped suddenly and stood upright after checking a box. 'This box has been tampered with and I think there are some items missing.'

David focussed his torch on the box. Using gloved hands, he checked the seal. 'It would appear it's been cut. Are you sure, Mr Haliwell, that this was sealed when you left last night?'

'I am certain. The stock came in a few days ago but is not due to go onto the shelves for another week. It's a catalogue special item for the third week of opening.'

'How would anyone know that they existed?' asked David.

'A customer could've picked up a catalogue in the store, or more likely saw it on our website,' said Bud. 'I saw it there myself and it clearly wasn't available until the week after next.'

'Jake, I need you in here,' called David. Jake appeared with is kit. 'Gabby can finish the door. I want you to print this box and record its contents. The manager seems to think it's been tampered with.'

'Done,' said Jake and began to dust the specific box and surrounding shelving and other boxes. He lifted a few prints and took several photographs.

'To check that all is okay, we will need to have fingerprints of all your employees, Mr Haliwell,' said David. 'We'll also need a log of the security panels by the back door.'

'Oh, you'll have to ask the security company for that,' said Bud. 'When will the prints have to be done?'

'We'll send someone to the store in the morning. Can you make sure that all who were working yesterday are available?' said David.

'I'll come back and do that, David,' said Anhton.

'If you're sure?'

'I don't live far from here, I can do it on my way in,' he said.

David turned back to Bud. 'Mr Haliwell, can you tell what it is that's missing?'

Yeah, a finely tuned and sensitive timer,' said Bud.

'What might they be used for?'

'Well, a number of different things, I guess. Timing for lighting set-ups. Added security in homes,' said Bud.

'What about bombs?' asked Jake

Everyone looked at Jake.

'Just asking?' said Jake.

'I suppose so, if someone had the right materials,' said Bud.

'Thank you, Mr Haliwell.'

5.3

Jake arrived and went straight to the Glass room so he could upload the new data from the previous night. Whilst he waited for Lassie to compile the data, he went to see Gabby.

'Good morning, my darling Gabby,' said Jake as he walked into her lab.

'Shut up,' she said. 'I've been here all night, thank you very much.'

'Well, excuuuuse me. I was out last night as well,' said Jake. 'Got anything for me on the stuff from last night?'

'How the hell did you find out about that already?'

'I was there.'

'Oh yeah. I need sleep.'

'Aww, poor baby.'

'Easy for you to say. You probably had Anhton keep you warm last night.'

'What? I did not!' said an indignant Jake.

'Well you should have. You make a good couple.'

'We are not a couple!'

'Oooh, did I hit a raw nerve?' said Gabby

'None of your business.'

'I did. You like him, don't you?'

'Maybe,' said Jake, going bright red.

'Nope, my hair is still redder than your face.' Gabby began to chuckle. 'Ask him out.'

'I can't.'

'Of course you can. I'm sure he'll say yes. I heard what he called you last night.'

'You weren't supposed to hear that,' said Jake.

'Well, I did.'

'What time do you knock off?'

'Two hours ago,' said Gabby.

'I'll come back at eleven then.'

'Out!'

Jake left the room laughing.

Taking the lift back to his floor, he bumped into Linda as he stepped off. 'Sorry about that.' He noticed she wasn't concentrating. 'What's the matter?'

'You're coming with me, and you're driving. I have to go and see if Derik's ok.'

'Derik?'

'Derik Scott, the reporter,' said Linda. 'The one who leaked that story to the news after we had that meeting with my old army unit.'

'Why are we seeing him suddenly?'

'When we came home, he married my oldest childhood friend. She rang me this morning saying she can't get hold of him.'

'Okay,' said Jake.

'Well, the suspected robbery last night is around the corner from their place. Yes, I've seen the preliminary report already.'

'What are we looking for then?'

'Derik,' said Linda.

They got into a DFIS Forden and Linda gave directions to Derik and Margie's place once they arrived at the electronics store.

'Are we allowed to just barge in?' asked Jake.

'Yes, Margie said to do what we had to do,' said Linda.

They parked out front and walked to the front door. There was no answer when they knocked, so Linda led Jake to the back. The back door was locked, so they checked the study Derik had set up in a shed in the back yard. That too was locked.

'I want to enter the house and look inside,' she said.

'Do we have to break in, or do you have a key?' said Jake.

Jake readied a pair of gloves as Linda began fossicking for a key.

'Here it is, just where Margie said it would be.'

She carefully opened the back door and they went inside. After searching each room, there was no sign of Derik anywhere. Nor were there any signs of a struggle.

'I'll call Gabby and have forensics go over the place,' said Jake.

Linda nodded.

Jake called Gabby, and after receiving an earful of abuse, he managed to get her to bring the van. Forty-five minutes later, Jake let Gabby and Amy in through the front door. They dusted the doors for prints and confirmed that there seemed to be no sign of a struggle. Nor did it appear that anyone had been in the house for at least twenty-four hours or more.

Jake went outside and searched the front and back yards but could not find anything unusual or that showed any signs of struggle. As a courtesy, he decided to bring any mail in for Linda's friend. When he opened the letterbox, he stopped and called for Linda.

'What do you make of this, Linda?' said Jake.

Linda peered inside and gasped loudly. 'This has now become personal. I want to find out who did this and why they're doing it. In case you haven't worked it out, that's the fourth member of my old army unit now unaccounted for. What the hell am I going to say to Margie?'

'Tell her the truth,' said Jake. 'Tell her Derik's missing. It's no use beating around the bush. She has the right to know. Tell her we're doing our damnedest to find out what's going on.'

'I know. First it was Damian, and then Vic. Then it was Garthen. Now it looks like Derik is missing. Who's next?'

Jake gave Linda a strong warm hug.

'Thanks, Jake. You're a gem.'

'That's okay,' said Jake. 'I'll get Gabby to get this back to the lab. Maybe there's a fingerprint on this one.'

'I doubt it somehow,' said Linda.

Jake went inside to get Gabby who followed him back outside to the letterbox. She meticulously photographed the position of the card, this time the six of diamonds. She then removed, tagged and bagged it before dusting the letterbox for prints. When Gabby came back to say they'd finished, she and Amy left the address. Jake and Linda closed the house and drove to DFIS HQ arriving about twenty minutes after Gabby and Amy.

Jake headed directly to the lab to see Gabby.

Gabby didn't even turn when Jake entered.

'Don't start,' she said, without turning around. She simply held up her hand for Jake to be silent.

Jake walked quietly across the room, placed a large, heavily sugared and flavoured drink next to her and backed away slowly.

'Stop where you are, mister.'

Jake stood and turned. Gabby raced across the room and threw her arms around him.

'Why do all the good ones have to be gay,' she said.

'What have I done now?' asked Jake, a little confused.

'Nothing. Thank you for being you,' said Gabby. 'I hope to have the results of these new items and the toy car from last night up to you in about an hour, provided I don't get disturbed again. Or fall asleep.'

'When you're done, you're done. I can wait.'

Gabby kissed him on the cheek, let him go and opened the door for him. Jake went back to his desk to see that Anhton had now arrived at his.

'What time do you call this?' said Jake.

'Working on the way to work,' said Anhton.

'Is that what they call it now?'

'Yes, it is.' Anhton dropped the paperwork on the desk and spread out several sheets of fingerprints.

Neither Jake nor Anhton noticed a figure slip into the office area and hide behind a partition near to their desks.

'That certainly looks like work to me. What are they?'

'The fingerprints of the shop assistants from the electronics store,' said Anhton. 'I said I'd drop by and gather them on my way to work today.'

'Don't you have electronic copies of them?' asked Jake.

'That can be arranged as well, but I thought this might help us get going.'

'This is true.'

Jake looked over the fingerprints.

'So, you think I'm sexy, hey?'

'I do,' said Anhton.

'Do you want to have dinner with me sometime?' asked Jake.

'I'd love that very much.'

'Cool.'

They both turned when they heard a squeal come from nearby and suddenly Gabby popped up from behind a partition.

'What were you doing there?' asked Jake.

'Listening to our conversation,' said Anhton.

Jake looked Gabby. She tried to look innocent.

She went up to Jake and hugged him tightly, then did the same to Anhton.

'Why are you acting so strange?' asked Jake.

'Well, you too are so cute together and I just knew something was going to happen,' said Gabby.

'Is that so?' said Jake.

'Gabby knows these things.'

'I gather you have some info for us?' asked Jake, changing the subject.

'Not so fast,' said Gabby. 'I want all the juicy details after you date.'

'Information, Gabby,' said Jake sternly.

'There's nothing new,' said Gabby. 'There's not a scrap of a fingerprint on the toy car or on either of the two cards.'

'That's no fun,' said Jake.

'Whoever is doing this, knows what they're doing,' said Gabby. 'The toys could've been bought anywhere. I'm going to check on my way home to see if I can get one similar to compare. As for the cards, they're standard stock. We even have that style of deck here. They may have come from the same deck as the others we've found, but until we find that deck, we won't know for sure. Sorry I couldn't be any more help.'

'Thanks, Gabby, you've done well,' said Jake.

'I'm going home to sleep,' said Gabby and left the office.

As Jake turned back to Anhton, he saw that Anhton was puzzled about something.

'What's the matter?' Jake asked.

'The playing cards that have been left?' said Anhton, 'Do they have a hole in them? A neatly cut hole.'

'I don't know,' said Jake. 'We can pull them up on Lassie and we'll have a look.'

Jake pressed the start button on the corner of the table. As soon as Lassie was ready, he loaded his report and data from the previous night, along with Gabby's report. Anhton also loaded his reports to Lassie.

'Now that we have that compiling, let's have a look at the cards,' said Jake. 'Lassie, can you please show all the playing cards that we have on file for this investigation?'

'One moment, Jake,' said Lassie.

Within a few seconds, the six cards appeared on the screen.

'There, look,' said Anhton, pointing to a part of the card in the lower left hand corner.

'I've never noticed that before,' said Jake.

'Lassie, this is Anhton ...'

'... I know your voice Anhton,' said Lassie.

'Oh. Okay. can you please overlay each card on top of each other?' asked Anhton.

'How's this?' said Lassie as the cards moved and were stacked over each other on the screen.

'Can you remove the layering option. I need to know if the hole in the bottom left corner of the card aligns with the ones above and below.'

The cards moved once more until it appeared that there was only one card.

'Can you change the background colour please, Lassie?' asked Anhton.

'What colour would you like?'

'Red should do it.'

'Red it is,' said Lassie.

The background screen changed to red and Anhton raised his finger to the hole on the top card.

'If the holes didn't line up then we would not be able to see the red background,' said Anhton.

'Yet there it is,' said Jake. 'A red dot on the card.'

'At least we know where the cards came from.'

'The casino.'

'The casino,' said Anhton.

'Wouldn't they punch a hole in the same place on each deck they discard?'

'We'll just have to ask and find out.' Anhton picked up his tablet and began to type.

Jake activated the keyboard on Lassie's table and also began to type.

'Lassie, you can revert the background to the previous setting and you can clear the cards away as well.'

'As you wish.'

'Let's see, each card has a hole in the lower left corner,' said Jake out loud as he typed. 'Each card lines up with the hole in the others cad that we have. that means they have come from the same deck, pending confirmation. The deck itself has been sold off by the casino.'

Jake stopped typing and sat back in his chair.

'That's done,' said Anhton. 'I've sent an email to the casino asking;

how often they sell off their decks?

if they do?

whether they punch the holes in the same place each time?

if not, do they keep a record of when they punch the decks in a certain place?

Then asking if they keep any record of who purchased the decks?'

At that moment, Linda and David walked into the Glass room.

'Do you have the results from Gabby?' asked David.

'Compiling the information now,' said Jake. 'As we suspected, there are no prints on the toy car or the cards.'

'Interesting,' said David.

'Where to now?' asked Linda.

'Funny you should ask,' said Jake. 'Why don't you tell them, Anhton.'

Linda and David looked at him.

'When I heard that there were no apparent prints on the cards, I was trying to think of how else we might look at this case. I came up with the idea to see if the cards had a hole in them.'

'You mean like when the casino sells off their decks after use?' said David.

'Exactly.'

'What did you find?' asked Linda.

'Holes. Perfectly matching holes on the cards we currently have.'

'Excellent,' said David.

'We're waiting for a response from the casino regarding those decks,' added Jake. 'We are now surmising that cards have come from the same deck sold off by the casino.'

'If Derik is now part of this, I want it resolved and the person put away,' said Linda. 'I reckon we're now dealing with the same person.'

'You mean from the theft of the D6 back in January to the suspected theft of the electronic timers last night?' asked David.

'What do you think, Jake?' said Linda. 'Are we dealing with the same person?'

'Yes I do, Ma'am,' stated Jake.

5·4

Jake and Anhton met to go tenpin bowling. They decided to do this for something different. Even though they had been working together for quite some time, this was the first time they were going on an official date. They'd gone past the awkwardness of discovering who each other was, they had Gabby to thank for that. As good a friend as Gabby had become with Jake, she was also as subtle as a brick sometimes.

They walked into the bowling alley. A number of the lanes were in use. Being a weeknight, they realised that there were leagues in action. After paying for their games and collecting their shoes, they made their way to their assigned lanes.

'Do you like big balls or small balls?' asked Jake.

Anhton nearly dropped his shoes where he stood. He turned slowly, his faced bright red and a daggery look in his eyes. He then saw Jake trying to suppress a smirk.

Anhton nodded once. 'Depends on what you've got for me?'

That stopped Jake in his tracks. However, he soon began to laugh. This drew looks from the leagues players they were passing.

'We might want to keep the innuendos to ourselves,' said Jake. 'We don't want to embarrass the neighbours.'

'You started it.'

'You played along. Just grab your ball and let's get going.'

'Oh you say the sexiest things sometimes,' said Jake.

Anhton groaned, hung his head and continued on to their lanes, which happened to be last in the alley.

They sat down and put on their shoes.

'I hope they've sprayed these,' said Jake.

'I'm sure they have.'

'Maybe I should buy my own pair?'

'And you bowl how often?' asked Anhton.

Jake smiled and stood up.

'You do realise that Gabby has been pushing for us to do this for months now?' said Jake.

'I kind of got that from her,' said Anhton. 'So why has it taken us this long?'

Jake looked at the ground. 'I didn't know if you'd say yes or not,' he mumbled to the ground.

'You thought I'd say no?'

'Yep.'

'What if I said yes?' said Anhton.

'I was still scared you'd say no.'

Anhton began to laugh.

'It's not funny,' said Jake.

'Yes, it is. I like you. I like you very much. If you hadn't asked, I was about to.'

'How long would you have waited?'

'As long as it took for you to grow a set,' said Anhton.

'I see.' Jake smiled broadly. He grabbed Anhton in the tightest hold he could. 'I'd kiss you now, but we're already getting strange looks.'

Jake let him go and they both laughed.

Jake and Anhton got set up on their lanes and began to bowl.

'You need to know something about me,' said Jake. 'I sometimes partake of certain actions and ponder whatever it is I'm working on. Usually I meditate, but sometimes I'll jog, or workout.'

'Tonight you're bowling?' said Anhton.

'Yes, which means rather than sit and meditate about work, I'll talk about it, with you.'

'Way to make a fun evening boring.'

'Thanks.'

Whilst he waited for his turn, Jake pondered the recent additions to the case.

'So, firstly we have the theft of the D6,' said Jake, after he sent his first ball down the alley.

'Might be used with a bomb.'

Jake retrieved his ball and sent it down again, having not secured the strike he wanted. 'Yes it could. Add to that the blasting caps and leads,' he said walking back to their seat.

'That would definitely spell bomb to me,' said Anhton,

as he lined up his first ball. Strike. 'Yes,' added Anhton, fist-pumping the air.

'Show off,' said Jake, as he prepared to send down his second ball. 'That was followed by the theft of the access cards.' Jake turned and poked his tongue out at Anhton. 'Strike, mister.'

'You look sooo adult when you poke your tongue out like that,' said Anhton, preparing to deliver his next ball. 'Not sure how the access cards fit into the bomb scenario, though.'

Anhton watched as his ball made its way down the alley. It hit the head pin front on, leaving him with a seven-ten split. 'Shit!'

'I'm sure we'll find out,' said Jake.

'What's next?' said Anhton, sending his second ball down and missing both the standing pins.

Jake took his time lining up his next ball. 'Bulls eye.' He turned back towards Anhton. 'Winner enjoys dinner at loser's expense for two weeks,' he added, holding out his hand.

Anhton took the bet.

'Next? That would have been last week with the theft of the electronic timers,' said Jake.

Anhton concentrated on his next ball. He too bowled a strike.

'Ha!'

'I'm still leading,' said Jake, leaning back on the seat. 'For my first meal, I like a full roast chicken dinner, cooked at home.'

'You like counting chickens before they hatch?'

'I'm going to win.'

Jake stood to bowl.

'Electronic timers could certainly be used with a bomb,' said Anhton.

Jake bowled his ball. He struck nine, leaving one remaining.

'That's all the items that have been taken so far,' said Jake. He sent the second ball of the frame down the alley. It was clean, smooth and clinical. The one remaining pin was flicked into the side wall. 'We also have to sort out the people missing, the items left behind as well as the playing cards. Oh, have you heard back from the casino yet?'

'Not yet. I'll give them a call tomorrow.' Anhton stood to bowl. He sent the ball down but it only knocked over seven pins.

'Ooops,' said Jake.

Anhton sent the second ball of the frame down the alley and only knocked over another two pins.

'Currently we have 2ndLt Damian Smithson, Vic Forde, Garthen Todorovic and Derik Scott all missing,' said Jake.

'Presumed dead?' asked Anhton.

'After this amount of time, we have to presume so.' Jake rose and collected his ball.

Strike.

'Nice bowl,' said Anhton.

'Thanks.'

Anhton sent his next down the alley.

Strike.

'Copy-cat I see,' said Jake.

'Not at all, just a good bowler.'

'Indeed. I'm still leading.'

'For the time being,' said Anhton. 'What else do we have?'

Jake rose to bowl.

'We have the items.'

Strike.

'Refresh me?' said Anhton, as he quickly lined up his next. Seven. 'Shit!'

'Ooops.'

'Refresh me?' repeated Anhton, as he sent the second ball on its way. Spare.

'We have a sunflower, a black parasol, an ink bottle, some small magnetic road signs and now a toy Austin Healey car.'

Jake bowled. Another spare, bowling a six and then knocking over the remaining four.

'I feel that there has to be something with the items left behind. I'll have another look at them on Lassie tomorrow.'

'They're so random though,' said Anhton.

'Yes they are, but they have to have a relationship with each other, otherwise why use them. Whoever is doing this wants us to work it out, but not easily.'

Anhton rose to bowl. 'What's next?'

'We have the playing cards,' said Jake.

Strike.

'The cards, what are they?'

'Ten of spades, nine of diamonds, eight of hearts, seven of clubs, six of spades and a six of diamonds,' said Jake.

Jake stood, grabbed his ball and began to line up the pins. With his arm ready to release the ball, he suddenly stopped, almost dropping the ball on his toes. 'Oh my god.'

'What's up?' said Anhton.

'It's a countdown.'

'What is?'

'The events that have taken place. I need to get to Lassie as soon as we're done here.'

'Then bowl, boyo,' said Anhton.

Although Jake won, his concern was to get to DFIS HQ as quickly as possible. They checked in at the desk. Jake tapped the walls of the elevator impatiently as they travelled to their floor. As soon as the doors opened, he ran across the room and activated Lassie.

'Evening, Jake,' said Lassie.

'Evening, Lassie,' replied Jake. 'I need to see all the cards that have been collected to date.'

'Sure thing.'

'Arrange them vertically by date.'

'Okay, Jake. Here they come.'

Jake watched as the images of the cards appeared one by one, listed in a row vertically.

'Oh my god,' said Jake. 'It *is* a countdown.'

'How can you be so sure?' asked Anhton.

'It's a gut feeling and they've never been wrong yet. When I was with the MPs for a while, I learned to trust my gut first. Even then it took others a while to come around, nearly every time I was right. I know I'm right this time too.'

'I hope so,' said Anhton.

'Okay, that'll do for now,' said Jake. 'I had to sort that out otherwise it would've bugged me all night, and we wouldn't want that, would we?'

Anhton looked at Jake and then smiled.

'You wanna stay the night?' asked Jake.

'Hell yeah.'

'Let's go,' said Jake. 'Lassie, thanks for your help. You can shut down now.'

'Goodnight, Jake.'

* * * * *

The next morning, Jake came bounding into the office. Linda noticed it immediately. Gabby, who was just leaving from another night shift, saw him and stopped him.

'I know who stayed at your place last night?' she said, bailing him up against an empty desk.

'I don't know what you mean,' said Jake.

'I know that look,' said Gabby. 'Yay for you. You dirty little root rat. I'll speak with you later.'

'Yes, you need to go home to bed. You're delirious.' Jake pushed his way past her and went to his desk.

Linda came over and sat on the edge of the desk.

'Did Anhton stay over last night?' she asked.

'I don't know what you mean.'

'You brought him in here last night. You were here for about fifteen minutes and when you left you were both smiling,' said Linda.

'How the hell did you know that?'

'Security footage,' said Linda.

'Fuck,' said Jake.

'I'm sure you did,' said Linda.

Jake looked at her sharply.

'I'm not as innocent as you think. Why do you think I'm with DFIS? I pick up things others miss.' Linda rolled up a chair. 'So, did you have a good night?'

'Yes.'

'Is that all?'

'Yes.'

'Okay. So why did you bring him here then?'

Jake lit up, got out of his seat, and went to Lassie. Puzzled by his sudden movement, Linda followed him. By the time they reached Lassie, she was just about fully booted up.

'Lassie, can you bring up the cards you showed me last night?' asked Jake.

'One moment.' A few seconds later the same vertical row of cards popped up on the screen with their discovery dates. 'There you go, Jake.'

'Thanks, Lassie,' said Jake. 'Look, Linda, it's a countdown.'

'It seems to look that way. Are you sure?'

'My gut says so.'

'I've heard that his gut instincts are rarely wrong,' said another voice from behind them. 'What have you got, Jake?'

Jake and Linda turned to see David standing at the edge of the space.

'Talk to me, Jake.'

'I was thinking about the information we had so far, after the latest was added the other day. I suddenly realised the numbers on the playing cards were getting smaller. I rushed in here last night and had Lassie bring them up as you see on the screen. Since January, the numbers on the cards have been counting down.'

'I've just noticed that the time between is also getting less,' added Linda.

Jake turned and looked. 'Lassie, can you calculate the time between each date in weeks?'

'One moment, Jake.' A bar appeared at the bottom of the large glass table as Lassie processed the information. 'Ready.'

Jake watched as the dates popped up next to the numbered cards. As each successive date appeared, a number appeared next to it.

'Look. Each date after the first incident in January is one week less than the previous,' said Jake. 'If this is true, then another event will take place five weeks from the last one.'

'Lassie, what day is each of the dates?' asked Linda.

'Processing,' said Lassie.

Another piece of info appeared.

'Wow. Each event has taken place on a Wednesday,' said Linda.

'The next event will take place on Wednesday, September 9,' said Jake. 'Great, we have a city of almost five million people that covers an area of too many square kilometres to think about. Finding the location will be like finding a needle in a haystack.'

'Then you had better get moving and find a pattern,' said Linda.

'I'll get on to it right away,' said Jake.

Jake turned his attention to Lassie. 'Lassie, can you bring up a map showing each location that an event has taken place?'

'Give me a few minutes and you'll see what you want,' said Lassie.

'Great.'

As Jake left the Glass room, he ran into Anhton.

'Hello you,' said Jake. He quickly looked around and with no one looking, Jake kissed Anhton.

Jake continued to the kitchenette where he and Anhton got coffees. When they came back to the Glass zone, a colour map of greater Melbourne was showing on the screen. A red 'X' marked the place where each of the five events had taken place. In a smaller window hanging off the 'X' was the information from each site. The item found, the numbered card and the date and details. On the table below the vertical screen, the list of cards was showing.

'Lassie, can you add the items found to the list on the table, please?' said Jake

'One moment.'

'Thanks,' said Jake, when he saw the names and pics of the items begin to display. He began to drag the names of the items so they sat next to the numbered cards.

'What're you thinking, Jake?' asked Anhton.

'I feel there's a clue in the items being left behind,' he said. 'They're not random, but specific.'

Anhton stood next to Jake and looked at the table. 'Lassie, can you make the first letter of each item double size and bold?'

'Done,' said Lassie.

'Let's see what we have,' said Jake. 'S.B.I.M.A. no, no, no, that's not right. Let's have another look.'

'What are you looking for, Jake?' asked Anhton.

'Perhaps we need to be a little less specific with the names.'

'What do you mean?'

'Let's go through item by item,' said Jake. 'Item one; a sunflower. Simple, no other descriptive words, only the word of what it is.'

'Agreed.'

'Item two; the black parasol. How about we simply list it as a parasol. Whilst black describes a feature of it, it does not describe 'It'.'

'Makes sense,' said Anhton.

'Item three; an ink bottle. Bottle would be its simplest form, but this one is a little more complicated. Describing it as an ink bottle gives it a specific purpose, like the parasol is specific and the sunflower.'

'I get it now.' That would make item four; the magnetic road signs simply road signs?'

'Shit, shit, shit' said Jake.

'What's up, Jake?' asked Anhton.

'With item five being the Austin Healey, we are left with *S.P.I.R.A.* How many letters can we place at the end of this phrase to form a word?'

They thought for a moment.

'I can only think of one,' said Anhton. 'Spiral.'

'That's it, Anhton,' Jake grabbed the sides of his face and unashamedly kissed him on the lips. 'What if we linked the events?'

'Could be.'

Jake stepped around the table and stood in front of the vertical glass wall. Placing his finger on the first red 'X' he traced a line to the second, third, fourth and fifth. 'Lassie, can you clean up these lines?'

'Let me see,' said Lassie. 'How does this look?'

Jake and Anhton watched as Lassie curved the lines. Jake and Anhton stared. It looked exactly like a spiral.

'Can you project a path using the data we currently have?' asked Jake.

Lassie began to work. Jake returned to stand beside Anhton as Lassie projected a wide dotted line from the last known point. 'That's the best I can do, Jake.'

'Hmm, it's very broad,' said Jake. He turned to the wall nearby and picked up a handset. 'Hey David, can you come to Lassie? ... Yes, bring the LCmdr.' He replaced the handset. Moments later, David and Linda walked into the Glass zone.

'What is it, Jake?'

'Anhton and I started to correlate the data we had. We had Lassie plot the positions of each of the events,' said Jake. 'As we looked further, we added the items to the cards.'

'We enlarged and darkened the first initial and it spelt what you see,' added Anhton. 'We asked to see all words that began with this sequence of letters and only two came up. The only applicable word was 'spiral'.'

'I then traced lines from event to event and had Lassie clean them up. A pattern emerged and I had Lassie project a possible path,' said Jake.

'As you can see, it's broad but at least we don't have

to look all over Melbourne for the next possible event,' said Anhton.

David looked closely at the table and the screen behind it. 'Well, I never. I thought it'd take you longer to work something out.'

'We don't have that much time,' said Jake. 'If the next event is due to happen in five weeks, we need to try and find out where, when and what.'

'We think we know when it will,' said Anhton.

'How can you be sure?' asked Linda.

'Look at the table here, Ma'am,' said Anhton. 'Each event has taken place on a Wednesday and each subsequent event is one week less than the previous. The cards helped Jake work that one out.'

'Great work,' said Linda. 'I can at least tell the powers we have something to go on. David, do you know who looks after that area?'

'I think that would be with Metro Central or Metro South,' said David, looking at the map.

'Okay, I'll give the commanders there a call and see what they can do,' said Linda. She turned and left.

'Great work you two,' said David. 'I'm really amazed that you sorted it so quickly.'

'It's not sorted yet, we still have to catch someone,' said Jake.

'Armed with this info, we have a better chance,' said David. 'Are we able to speculate what the target might be?'

'I don't think so, but we can try and work something out,' said Jake.

6.1

The Brighton Star Hotel was a quiet place during the week. A few streets away, a matte-black tow truck found a place to park. Silently slipping in next to the curb, the engine was shut off. The light breeze made the shadows seem like they were moving. The dull moonlight added an eeriness to the area.

In the almost empty car park behind the Brighton Star Hotel, only two vehicles were parked. One near the rear entrance and the other, a white Forden AV, on the far wall, conveniently parked under a sign. What little lighting was in the car park was soon extinguished as wires were cut and then covered in black electrical tape to make it seem like nothing was wrong. In the near blackness, the shadow continued to move about the car park.

A few minutes later, the matte-black tow-truck silently pulled away from the curb. Once it had turned a corner, most of its running lights were activated and what must have been an enhanced muffler system, was switched off. The truck now sounded like a truck.

Screeching around another corner and into the car park, it backed up to the Forden. A single flash lit up the area around the vehicle and the wall it was parked against. The truck backed up a little closer to the Forden and soon it was hooked onto the back and secured. A large matte-black tarp was dragged over the car and tied in place. Just before the truck moved away, three items were hung from the sign on the wall.

Screeching its tyres once more, the truck left the car park of the hotel to a few houses switching on their lights at the noise. All they saw was a large truck with a covered load behind it. Lights so bright it blotted out the signage and licence plates. Once on the freeway, the truck's lights were dimmed and the enhanced muffler re-engaged. Travelling with minimal lighting, the truck was driven to a warehouse in the inner west of Melbourne. Navigating a laneway, the truck entered the rear door of a large warehouse building.

Travelling to the basement, three levels below, the truck parked near the middle of the floor. The Forden was lowered, uncovered and unlocked using the access codes and cards previously acquired. Once started, the Forden was parked in a corner. Over the next few minutes, the codes were changed and one of the access cards keyed to that vehicle only. This was left in the glove box and the Forden was covered, awaiting its makeover.

In the far left corner, a door opened and closed.

6.2

Two men entered the front door of the Metro East Police station arguing.

'You will explain to them what you did,' said the older man, as he followed the younger man into the building. 'You had no right to do what you did without checking with me first, and to go to a local hotel to drink. Shameful.'

'I'm sorry, father,' said the younger man.

'Can I help you gentlemen?' asked the office behind the counter.

'I wish to speak to a detective,' said the older man.

'Can I ask what it's about please?' asked the officer.

'I will tell the detective. I don't want just anyone to know what's happened,' said the older man. 'Please get me a detective.'

'Anything I can do to help, Jones?' said a senior female officer, addressing the officer at the counter.

'This gentleman has asked to speak to a detective but does not wish to tell me what it's about,' said the male officer.

'Thank you, Jones,' said the senior officer.

'I'm Sgt Melissa Caulfield, what is it you'd like to speak to a detective about?' she asked.

The older man looked the Sgt up and down. 'I will speak only with a detective.'

'For me to get a detective,' said Melissa, 'I need to know what the situation is.'

The older man looked puzzled. The younger man sniggered and received a clip over the ear.

'I'll thank you, sir, not to do that in front of a police officer,' said Melissa.

'I'll do as I please to my son,' replied the older man.

'Anything further and I will charge you with assault.'

'How dare you speak to me like that. I have diplomatic immunity.'

'Not on an issue of domestic violence you don't. The rules have changed, sir,' said Melissa. 'Now, what do you wish to speak with a detective about?'

The older man looked at her furiously. Melissa stood behind the counter and waited. The standoff lasted a few minutes.

'Well?' said the older man.

'Well, what?' said Melissa.

'Are you going to get a detective for me?'

'Are you going to tell me what it is you wish to speak to the detective about?'

'That's none of your business,' said the older man.

'You are in my police station, sir, that makes it my business.'

'I lost his diplomatic vehicle, Ma'am,' said the younger man.

'Thank you, I will get a detective for you,' said Melissa.

The older man turned and glared at the younger one.

This time the younger stood his ground, knowing that if he was struck again, he'd be safe.

Melissa left the front office and walked down the hall. She knocked on the door of a detective.

'Come in,' said the voice behind the door.

Melissa opened the door, stepped inside and stopped.

'Morning, Mel, what can I do for you?' asked the detective.

'Anhton, what are you doing here? I heard you were at DFIS,' said Melissa.

'I am, but I was needed here due to the shortage. Now you know. What's up?'

'Well, firstly, I want you to restrain me from bitch-slapping a foreign diplomatic pig.'

'Sounds like you've had a good morning then,' said Anhton, smiling.

'I'll bitch-slap you if you don't watch out.'

'What's up with our diplomatic friend?'

'He wouldn't tell me what he wanted to speak to a detective about, but eventually his son, I presume, said that he'd lost their diplomatic vehicle.'

'How do you lose a car?' asked Anhton.

'I don't know, he wouldn't tell me. I was lucky to get that out of him.'

'Show him to an interview room and tell him I'll be along soon.'

'I wouldn't wait too long at all, he might get a bit shirty with you,' said Melissa.

'He can cool his heels for a little while. Offer him some tea or coffee. I'm almost done here.'

'Sounds good to me.'

Melissa left the office and showed the two men to a small room. She offered them a drink, but only the younger man accepted.

About fifteen minutes later, Anhton entered the room.

'Good morning, my name's Det. Anhton Roberts. How can I help you today?'

The older man smiled warmly, stood and returned Anhton's handshake. 'I'm Count Dragomir Razmovski, envoy to Australia from the Principality of Morroconaya, and this is my son, Dragan.'

'I'm pleased to meet you both. How can I help you?'

'You can find the car my son lost,' said Dragomir.

'Where did you lose it, Dragan?' asked Anhton.

'I think it was stolen,' said Dragomir.

'Mr Razmovski sir, please, I need to hear the story from Dragan.'

Dragomir clipped Dragan around the back of the head again.

'Please, sir, there is no need for that,' said Anhton.

Dragomir looked sharply at Anhton.

'Is there a problem, Mr Razmovski?' asked Anhton.

'I thought you would understand discipline, detective.'

'There is discipline and there are unnecessary actions.'

'I am not abusing my son, detective!' stated Dragomir.

'What you do at home is completely your business, but in the presence of the law, you will refrain from such actions. They may cause you more harm than good.' Anhton looked calm. 'Now, Dragan, tell me what happened.'

Dragan looked at his father, who nodded. 'I went out to a local hotel in Brighton to meet some friends.

'Such lunacy. Young people should not be drinking at this age,' said Dragomir.

'Mr Razmovski, please, I want Dragan to tell me what happened without interruption. If you interrupt again, I will have you escorted to another room to wait. Please continue, Dragan. Which hotel in Brighton?'

'The Brighton Star, sir,' said Dragan.

'You can call me Anhton, I don't mind.'

Dragomir tutted and Anhton looked at him.

'Then what happened?' asked Anhton.

'I had a few drinks with my friends.'

'How many is a few?'

'Enough that I shouldn't drive home.'

Anhton smiled and that eased Dragan.

'I caught a taxi home and intended to return to the hotel the following morning to collect the car. I slept late and when I arrived at the hotel, it was gone. I went inside and asked but they couldn't help me.'

'We can get the information, I'm sure.'

In a room on the other side of a one way mirrored window, people began to move.

'What's going on here?' asked a female.

'Morning Det.Sgt,' said Melissa. 'Anhton is interviewing a diplomatic pig about a missing car that his son lost.'

'Now, now Mel, I'm sure he's not that bad,' said the Det. Sgt.

'Yes he is, Amita,' said Melissa.

'Okay. What do we know so far?' asked Amita.

'The son went to the Brighton Star hotel to meet friends. Drank too much and left the car at the hotel. When he went back it was gone. The hotel said they couldn't help.'

'Perhaps we'd better go down and see what we can do then,' said Amita. 'Does the boy think it's stolen?'

'No, but I reckon that's what happened,' said Melissa.

'Can you send a couple of uniforms down there and check out what they know?'

'Sure. I'll get on it right away,' said Melissa, and left the room.

'What else can you tell me, Dragan? When did this happen?'

'Last Wednesday night,' said Dragan.

'Why have you taken so long to come forward?'

'My father didn't return from an overseas trip until late last night. He found out this morning and here we are.'

'You should've come to us immediately. It will be much harder to check the scene, especially if the car has been stolen.'

'I'm sorry, sir. I know I should've, but I was embarrassed.'

'Not to worry, we'll send someone down to investigate. If we took you back there, could you remember where in the car park you left the car?'

'I think so.'

'Good,' said Anhton. 'Wait here please.'

Anhton rose and left the room. Amita met him in the hall.

'Hi, Amita. Have you heard what's been going on?'

'Yeah. I've asked Mel to send some officers to the hotel to make some inquiries. Do you think the car was stolen? Or did he park it elsewhere?'

'I don't think he parked it elsewhere and most likely it's been stolen,' said Anhton. 'I'd like to take the son back to the hotel to show me exactly where he parked the car. Hopefully there'll be something there for us.' Anhton stopped suddenly. 'I'll be right back.' He rushed back into the interview room. 'Dragan, are you sure about the day last week you were at the Brighton Star hotel?'

'Yes, it was last Wednesday, September 6,' said Dragan.

'Okay, thanks.'

'Is there a problem?'

'No, I just had to make sure.'

He left the room again.

'What was that about?' asked Amita.

'The date, I needed to check the date,' said Anhton.

'What's the date got to do with anything?' said Amita.

'It'll fit the pattern that Jake came up with over at DFIS.'

'Can't we handle this?' said Amita, dropping her shoulders.

'You're right. We don't know for sure that the missing Forden is linked with the DFIS case,' said Anhton. 'Do we have people we can send over to the hotel to investigate?'

'Do what you have to, Detective,' said Amita. 'I want to be kept up-to-date with anything that happens, even if we have to hand off to DFIS.'

'Yes, Ma'am,' said Anhton.

'What are you going to do?'

'Right, I'd like to take Dragan only to the hotel so he can tell me where he left the car.'

'Won't his father protest?' asked Amita.

'I have no doubt, but the boy will speak much easier and freer without his father telling him what to say or do,' said Anhton. 'We can leave him in the interview room and have Mel keep tabs on him.'

'From what I've heard, I don't think that's wise.' Amita smiled.

'In that case, I will instruct the father to go home,' said Anhton. 'I'm going in.'

'Good luck,' said Amita.

Anhton returned to the interview room. 'Thank you for being so patient.' Dragomir began to rise. 'Before you say anything, I want you to understand that what I'm about to tell will happen the way we want. Any obstructions and we will be caused to hold people longer than necessary.'

'You cannot treat a diplomat like this,' protested Dragomir.

'As this is a domestic enquiry, diplomatic immunity does not apply. Now, Dragan will be coming with me alone to the site where he parked the car.' Dragomir began to protest. 'It will be much easier, sir.' Dragomir tried to protest again. 'I will call you personally, or speak with you, when I return Dragan home,' said Anhton. 'Please trust me, we don't have much time anymore.'

'What do you mean?' asked Dragomir.

'I'm not at liberty to speak about the investigation,' Anhton turned to Dragan. 'Are you ready to go?'

'Yes I am, detective,' said Dragan.

'Let's go,' said Anhton. 'Mr Razmovski, if you will follow us, I can show you to the front office.'

Dragomir and Dragan rose and followed Anhton to the foyer. Anhton checked out a car and led Dragan to the basement car park, whilst Dragomir left the building looking confused. Anhton drove to the hotel and pulled into the car park.

'Where did you park the car that night?' asked Anhton.

'Over there,' said Dragan, pointing, as they drove through the car park.

The spot where the car had been parked was currently empty, so Anhton parked his car to block anyone using it. He got out and had a look at the parking space. Nothing seemed out of the ordinary on the ground. No glass or signs of anything having been broken. He looked at the wall, then up at the sign, and stopped. Hanging from the bottom of the sign was a five of hearts playing card, along with a plastic bag containing a doll's house sized lounge suite. Anhton's head dropped. Reluctantly pulling out his phone, he called Jake.

'What's' going on here?' called a gruff voice from across the car park.

Anhton turned to see a burly man striding in his direction. The two uniformed officers following along behind him.

Anthon spoke to the officers first. One went back to their squad car and returned with some police tape.

'Oi, you, I demand to know what's going on!' said the burly man.

'Good morning, sir. I'm Det. Anhton Roberts, and this parking space is now a crime scene,' said Anhton, showing the man his badge. 'You are?'

'Edan Chester, manager of the hotel,' said the man. 'What do you mean crime scene?'

'We believe that a car was stolen from this space last Wednesday night,' said Anhton. 'I will need your security tapes so that we can check what went on in the car park that night.'

'I don't have to hand over anything.'

'A court order will fix that pretty quickly and if anything has been tampered with, you will be held in contempt.'

The hotel manager huffed and walked off. Anhton had one of the police officers go with him, just in case he handed over the tapes immediately.

About thirty minutes later, Jake rolled up, along with David. Pulling up behind them was the DFIS forensics van.

'What you got?' said Jake.

'A car went missing last Wednesday from the space we have cordoned off,' said Anhton. 'I've had a brief look, but couldn't see anything on the ground, but the same calling cards are hanging from the sign.'

Jake wandered over, passed under the tape and looked at the items hanging from the sign. 'Ah, Gabby, some more toys for you to play with,' called Jake, as Gabby walked towards him with a case in one hand.

'I don't hold out any hope though, Jake,' she said.

Amy had already started taking photographs. 'There's not a lot to go on,' she said. 'The trail will be cold by now.'

'I'm sure it is,' said Jake. 'Do what you can.'

'You know I will, Jake,' said Amy.

'We're probably gonna have to talk to residents to see what they know,' said Jake, walking back to where Anhton stood.

'Probably,' said Anhton. 'Jake, this is Dragan Razmovski, the young man who had the car that night.'

They shook hands.

'Are you sure this is the space where you parked the car?' asked Jake.

'Yes, it was, sir.'

'Okay, we'll see what we can do,' said Jake.

'You've got the bloody tapes from last week now,' said Edan, as he strode over to Anhton.

Anhton looked around to see that David was holding them and placing them into an evidence bag. He then noticed that the hotel manager was looking puzzled.

'What's the matter, Mr Chester?' asked Anhton.

'That sign hanging on the wall over there, that's not a council sanctioned sign,' he said.

'What do you mean?' asked Anhton.

'The parking limits sign, that's not the one I ordered,' said Edan.

Anhton and Jake had a closer look at the sign. 'I think he's right,' said Anhton. 'Look at the very bottom, Jake.'

Jake looked closer and across the bottom were the numbers ten down to six followed by a series of dots leading to where the new card hung. 'Can we take this sign?' asked Jake.

'I don't care what you do with it, it's not mine,' said Edan. 'Now I have to go and buy a bloody new one.' Edan headed back to the hotel. 'Bloody stupid thugs. Think this is a freakin' joke.'

'Something else for you, Gabby,' said Jake. 'You'll need to take the sign as well.'

Gabby took the sign down carefully and placed it in a large evidence bag.

'What do we do now?' asked Anhton.

'I'll get some grunts over here and arm them with the information we have and see what the locals saw, if they remember,' said Jake.

'Leave that to me,' said Anhton. 'I'll get that sorted for you.'

'If you're sure?' asked Jake.

'Amita won't be happy, but she just has to lump it,' said Anhton. 'I'll call you as soon as I have anything.'

'Sounds great,' said Jake.

'Right, I had better get this young man back to his impatient father,' said Anhton. 'I'll let you know when I have anything from the locals. Also, I'll get the car rego details for you too.'

'Deal. I'll have a closer look around here, just in case there's something we missed,' said Jake.

Anhton left with Dragan and Jake stepped under the tape.

6.3

'Found anything at all, Amy?' asked Jake.

'I'm not sure, but there are marks here that look almost like skid marks,' she said.

'Whereabouts?'

'Here.' Amy waved her hand over a few marks on the pavement.

Jake got down on his knees and could see them a bit better. 'Have you got the happy snaps of these?'

'Yep, just in case.'

'Let's see if we can make anything out of the marks once we have the results of the neighbourhood door knock,' said Jake.

'I reckon we've gathered as much as we can get for now,' said Gabby.

'Okay then, let's get back to base and see what we get from the toys and card,' said Jake. 'David, can you handle staring through a few hours' worth of tape?'

'Do we have a specific date and time?' he asked.

'Last Wednesday, dunno about the time,' said Jake.

'Last Wednesday, wasn't that when the next event was to take place?' he asked.

'Yep,' said Jake. 'This event, actually.'

'How are we supposed to stop these events?'

'By working damned hard,' said Jake.

'Where do we begin?'

'Let's see what Gabby has for us. Perhaps she can find something. Then let's hope the tapes throw something useful up as well'

'We can try,' said David.

Jumping in their cars, the DFIS crew headed back to their HQ in Newport. Jake parked in the basement and they took their gear to Lassie to upload the latest data. Once they had that done, they waited for Lassie to finish compiling and putting up the requests Jake asked for.

'I think you're right, Jake,' said David.

'About?'

'The countdown down and the fact that the events are spiralling. Look at the new item added.' He pointed to the list of items and their names with the highlighted first letter.

'How does the D from doll fit in though?' asked Jake.

'Actually, I think we've got that one wrong.' David consulted his tablet. 'Lassie, can you change the name of the latest item to 'Lounge suite' please?'

'Yes I can, David. One moment.'

When Jake and David looked at the vertical screen, it made sense.

'See, S P I R A and now L.

- S-unflower card,

- P-arasol,

- I-nk bottle,

- R-oad signs,

- A-ustin Healey, and now,

- L-ounge suite.

Spiral. Just as you said.'

'Yet we still couldn't catch the perp,' said Jake.

'You had the area right, but how could we know what the perp was going to do.'

'It's so frustrating though. Eight months and nothing.'

'We know that it has to be the same person,' said David. 'The items being left behind are too similar for them to be left by someone else.'

'Okay, what's the next target zone and how long do we have?'

'You worked that out last time, what do you think?'

'Lassie, using a similar trajectory that we used to calculate the spiral extension from Burwood down to Brighton, can you give me a rough idea of the area most likely to be covered with a new extension of the spiral?'

'That may take a few minutes, Jake,' said Lassie.

'We'll go and get a coffee and be back,' said Jake.

'I need to speak with Linda,' said David. 'Let me know what happens with the results.'

Jake nodded. As he entered, he saw the plastic wrapped plates of sandwiches and cakes.

'Guys, you didn't have to celebrate my return from the field with such a feast,' said Gabby as she entered the kitchen.

'We didn't,' said Jake. 'What's wrong with your kitchen?'

'Too boring. There's more life in a drop of distilled water than down there.'

Jake laughed.

'I hope you're not getting in early,' said David, entering the kitchen.

'What's all this about, sir?' asked Jake.

'We have a guest here today,' David replied.

'How come we weren't informed?'

'We only found out this morning,' said David. 'We only had enough time to get this lunch quickly.'

'Who's the guest?' asked Linda.

'The chief of security for the President-elect,' said David.

'Dawn's here?' said Jake.

'Yes, Dawn Forde is here today. She's with the Cmdr right now. I think she wants to know what's happening with the case that includes her missing partner, Vic Forde,' said David. 'I hope your case notes are in order?'

'They are, sir. We were just adding the latest information from our trip to Brighton this morning.'

Linda escorted Dawn into the lunchroom.

'Please forgive our informal lunch facilities, Dawn, but we didn't have a great deal of notice today,' said Linda.

'That's okay, Linda, I wasn't expecting a formal reception,' replied Dawn.

Linda introduced those in the room to Dawn.

'Crpl North, I've heard good things about you,' said Dawn.

'Thank you, Ma'am,' said Jake.

'Dawn is quite okay, Crpl,' said Dawn.

'Then Jake is fine as well.'

'What progress have you made on the countdown case?'

'Briefly, we now know that the events have been happening in a spiral. I have Lassie calculating the next event zone,' explained Jake. 'Would you like to see what we have?'

'Yes, I would. Thank you.'

Jake showed Dawn to the Glass zone, explained how it worked and then showed her the progress to date. Everyone looked astonished as the new event zone took shape. Right in the middle of the zone was Newport. When it was enlarged, the new DFIS HQ was almost in the middle of it.

'That wasn't quite expected,' said Jake. 'Lassie, are you sure of the projected event zone?'

'Yes, I am, Jake. I have calculated the projected area according to the specs you used to join the rest of the dots.'

'I see.' Jake turned to David and Linda. 'I'll check the calculations later, David, to make sure.'

'David tells me that you can also predict the date of the next event?' asked Dawn.

'Again, I'm using the previous events to help me with that. So far, each subsequent event is one week less than the previous,' said Jake.

'When is this next one due to take place?'

'Wednesday October 7,' said Jake.

Silence enveloped the room.

6.4

Dawn was just finishing getting dinner ready when Jeremy came home with her two boys. Jeremy was staying with Dawn often and the boys loved the company as well. They got on well with Jeremy.

Jeremy greeted Dawn with a huge kiss.

'Did the boys have fun today?' asked Dawn.

'I think so,' said Jeremy. 'I showed them my car collection.'

'I didn't know you collected cars?'

'I only started since coming back. It's helped me with the stress.'

'Do you restore them?' asked Dawn.

'Some of them I do. I showed them my pride and joy.'

'Which is?'

'A 1958 Austin Healey 100/6 Cabriolet,' said Jeremy.

'Yes, the boys would've loved it. They love cars.' Dawn turned back to her dinner preparations.

'Hey, I was gonna do dinner for you tonight,' said Jeremy.

'I finished early, so thought I'd make it for a change,' Dawn replied.

'Okay. How was your day?'

'Busy. Informative.'

'Oh, what did you learn?'

'DFIS are making progress on the Spiral case.'

'The spiral case?'

'It's what I've called it anyway.'

'Can you tell me anything?'

'Now, you know I can't talk about work that much,' said Dawn.

'I had to ask. It's not fair you mentioning a case name but not being able to say much else.'

'Get used to it,' said Dawn.

'No details then, just an outline.'

Dawn turned in his arms and looked at him. She felt she could trust him. He looked at her deeply. They kissed passionately.

'When's dinner?' said a voice from the kitchen door.

'Soon, my love. It's almost ready,' said Dawn, as she turned back to the cooking.

Jeremy walked to the patio door and stared across the back yard. 'I might go in to DFIS tomorrow and see if they can tell me anything themselves.'

'Why do you want to know, dear?' asked Dawn.

'Some of my former army colleagues are missing, including Vic and Damian, and I'd like to know what's going on. I told you they called us in after Garthen went missing and advised we look out for ourselves. Well, now Derik's missing as well, so I'm wondering who's next.'

'Fair enough, I guess,' said Dawn. 'You will tell me what's happening then, won't you?' She smiled wryly.

Jeremy turned to catch the smile and smiled back at her.

Dawn saw an emotion flick across his face that made her take a second look.

6.5

Jake came home from DFIS HQ, frustrated that he couldn't find anything that might lead him to the person who was committing all these crimes. It was definitely a serial offender but they couldn't be labelled as a serial killer, as no bodies have been found to prove that. They can't be labelled a serial thief, even though things have obviously gone missing. They are definitely a serial plotter, but what was it they were plotting.

Jake put his satchel on the dining room table, changed into some jogging gear, locked his townhouse and went for a long jog.

I know that the word is now 'spiral' and that usually means it's spiralling towards the centre. You would think with the word finished, so would the crimes, however my gut is telling me otherwise.

So far everything has happened on a Wednesday night, so if there is another event, it will be the same. As the dates countdown, what does the timeline look like? Now, if we are dealing with a countdown, what are we counting down too.

If last week's event was five weeks after the previous, that would mean that the next event is only four weeks away. Seeing as we are one week into that time already, that only leaves three weeks left to the next. Add three more weeks for the event after that, followed by another two, then one, we have nine weeks from now.

Now I will have to check my calendar as to what's happening in nine weeks.

Jake ran some more. The nine-week time frame played over and over in his head. *What's happening in nine weeks?*

Jake thought furiously. Suddenly he stopped.

'Oh, fuck, no.'

He took off at a rapid pace and reached his front door in less than half the time it had taken him to get to his turning point. He grabbed his tablet as he caught his breath. He impatiently waited for it to start up, and when it had, he opened the calendar feature and worked out what was happening in nine weeks.

'This can't be happening,' he said. 'We have to stop this and stop it now.'

6.6

A smartly dressed woman made her way along the tiled corridor. The clip of her heels echoed as she walked.

She turned a corner and stepped onto the much quieter carpet that was the outer office.

'Morning, Ms. Moors,' said the receptionist.

'Morning, Rachel,' replied Ms. Moors. 'Is he in?'

'He's waiting for you. Go right in.'

'Thank you.'

Ms. Moors opened the solid wood door, stepped through and closed it behind her.

'Good morning, Ethan,' said Ms. Moors, stretching out her hand.

Ethan Abernathy, 67, 186cm tall, athletic, greying hair, light hazel eyes and well cared for skin. Due to his fitness regime, he came across as being a much younger man.

'Ah, good morning to you too, Bryony,' said Ethan, returning her handshake. 'What have you got for me today?'

'Only one matter. We seem to have lost contact with one of our operatives.'

'Indeed. How did this happen?'

'He came to us through one of our other contacts, a Jeremy Pyke, and since that contact, we've dealt directly with this person,' said Bryony. 'No one has ever met them, so we're not sure if they are male or female. Our repeated attempts at contact have gone unanswered.'

'We've been tracking them though?'

'We have, and the signal always stops at one particular place. We've watched the place but not seen anyone come and go. Either they know we're there, or come and go when we're not.'

'I see,' said Ethan. 'What's the latest then?'

'The last movement we had was some weeks ago when we tracked the phone to a place on the coast just past Altona.'

'Not much along there. The result?'

'We took a car out but the trail ended at private property,' said Bryony. 'There seems to have been activity recently, but so as not to attract too much attention, we drove away. I know private property has not stopped us in the past, but we really didn't know how we'd answer queries.'

'Then?'

'We took a craft and flew over the property. All that we saw was a burnt out shed on the edge of the water. We couldn't stay long as we were then herded away by the air wing. It seems to have ended with that contact.'

Ethan rose and stood by the window. 'What of this Jeremy Pyke? Can we contact him again?'

'We have yet to do this. We think he might be suffering from PTSD as he is usually quite short with us when we do speak with him.'

'Is he a threat to Calderwood?'

'No,' said Bryony. 'He's never been here and doesn't know what we do. He's more of an information contact. Someone we go to only when we need certain information about someone or something. We don't use him that often.'

'Okay, we'll leave him be for now. Keep an eye on him all the same.'

'No one is ever off our radar, Ethan.'

Ethan turned, smiled at Bryony and sat down. 'Thank you, Bryony.'

'Yes, Ethan. Have a good day.' Bryony turned and left the office.

7.1

Jake and David arrived at DFIS HQ at the same time. One by one they parked beside each other in the underground car park. They noted that Linda's car was here as well, she'd arrived before them for a change. Greetings were jovial as they rode the lift to their floor.

As they got out, their moods changed when they saw Linda standing in the Glass room, arms folded and all the data they'd collected visible on the screen. They put their satchels on their respective desks and walked to the Glass zone.

Jake, who had been doing most of the work, felt the weight of failure fall on his shoulders.

'I was reviewing all the work we've been doing so far,' said Linda. 'Apart from no result, I am still very impressed.'

'It's been difficult, Ma'am,' said Jake. 'The person committing all these crimes knows what they're doing and we haven't been able to get a single print off anything left behind.'

'Absolutely nothing?'

'I can get Gabby to go over them all again. She may have missed something.'

'That'll be okay, Jake. I know Gabby, she won't have missed a thing,' said Linda. She turned back to the Glass. 'You think that the target event is Independence Day, Jake?'

'Yes, I do Ma'am,' said Jake confidently.

Linda turned and looked at him. 'You seem so sure about that?'

Jake stepped put to the Glass. 'Lassie, please highlight the dates of each event beginning with the first one in January.'

'Processing now, Jake,' said Lassie.

'This shouldn't take long,' said Jake.

'Here you go,' said Lassie.

The six events were highlighted and enlarged on the vertical screen. Each date was made bold.

'As you can see, each event took place at night on a Wednesday. Albeit some moved into the early hours of Thursday morning, but it's still often considered as Wednesday night. Each date, apart from the first one, is one week less than the time before.

'What do you mean?' asked Linda.

'Sure,' said Jake. 'Event 1 took place on Wednesday January 8. Event 2 took place on Wednesday March 11, which is nine weeks after event one. Event 3 was Wednesday May 6, eight weeks after event two. This continues right up to event six which took place on Wednesday September 6, five weeks after event five. Therefore, if the pattern holds true, the next event should be on Wednesday October 7, which will be four weeks after event 6 and is due to happen tonight.'

'Yes, now I understand. So how did you arrive at the target being Independence Day?'

'Again, following the pattern, the next event after this one will take place on Wednesday October 28, three weeks from today. The next event after that is a further two weeks later, on Wednesday November 11 and the final event is the following week, Wednesday November 18.'

'Independence Day,' said Linda.

'Independence Day,' said Jake.

'Do we know where this will take place?'

'Somewhere in the CBD,' said Jake.

'How did you figure that one?'

'Firstly, we noticed a pattern occurring with the items that were being left behind,' said Jake.

'You didn't discover that one?' asked Linda.

'No, I didn't, David did.'

'Well done, David.'

'Thanks, Ma'am,' said David. 'Then Jake joined the dots to get the connection we've been working from.'

'When we began to plot the locations of the events, the spiral pattern emerged,' said Jake. 'Whilst the perp has been clean, he has been telling us all along what he's doing. That's the most infuriating part.'

'I know I've been shown this along the way, I haven't been reading about it every day,' said Linda.

Jake nodded.

'Now, David tells me that Newport is the next potential target zone for the next event?'

'It could be anywhere from Williamstown to Spotswood or even all the way out to Altona and Laverton.'

'Have we notified anyone about this yet?'

'As Cmdr Peter Dugald, the Williams base commander, was a member of the disbanded army unit that Damian, Vic, Garthen and Derik, and of course you, were a part of, he has been privy to the information,' said David. 'He is aware of the potential target zone and is taking precautions.'

'What about us?' asked Linda.

'We have put the HQ on alert as well.'

'Very good.'

'Is there anything else I can help you with, Ma'am?' asked Jake.

'Not any more, Crpl. I have all the info I need now,' said Linda. 'Thank you very much.'

Jake and David watched Linda walk back to her office. For a moment, she stood and looked back to the Glass zone.

'I'd better go,' said David, 'I think I'm wanted.'

For the remainder of the morning, Jake worked on the case. He went over the clues again to see if they'd missed anything. Jake dragged a desk into the Glass zone, took off his shoes, sat on top, crossed his legs and began to breathe rhythmically. He focussed on the information in front of him, closed his eyes and began to medicate.

Four members of the same army unit, missing, presumed dead. Are they the targets? Were they simply in the wrong place at the wrong time? Then why steal all the other stuff. 5kg bag of 6, several blasting caps, blasting leads, an electronic timer. All components stolen indicate the making of a bomb? Forden AV access cards and codes. Diplomatic Forden AV. Why steal an AV? That would explain why the access cards were stolen. Are they going to use the stolen Forden to carry the bomb? What is the final target? Independence Day celebrations?

After thirty minutes, he stopped, stretched his legs and walked back to his desk.

'Any luck?' asked Gabby who was leaning back in the at the desk opposite, her feet leisurely resting on the desk.

'Not really,' said Jake. 'Besides, my stomach started to rumble. Why are you here?'

'What is that smell?' said Gabby, rudely sniffing the air. She looked under Jake's desk. 'It's you!'

'It is not.'

'Your shoes are under the desk. They are not on your feet. It's you.'

'They were clean this morning,' said Jake.

'With emphasis on the word 'morning' I might add.'

'They were clean.'

Gabby laughed. 'I'm here to take you to lunch.'

Jake stepped from the lift to a heated discussion coming from behind closed doors in Linda's office. He paused where he was to listen.

'Danika, you have to trust me,' pleaded Linda. 'Our facts are pointing to something happening on Independence Day.'

'Please forgive me, Linda, but I have taken your facts with a grain of salt,' said Danika. 'You haven't caught anyone with these facts, and it appears another member of our unit is missing. Do you know where Derik is?'

'I'm asking you as a friend to consider the facts.'

'The only reason I'm here is because Dawn insisted. Ex-army and all, otherwise it would be much different. Unless you can give me hard evidence, I cannot and will not make any changes to Independence Day proceedings.'

Just then David stepped from the lift, bumped into Jake, which pushed him into the line of sight of Linda. She came bounding out of her office.

'Jake, can you please show the President-elect the evidence we have pointing to an event taking place on Independence Day?'

Linda pushed Jake into the Glass room, with Danika following, arms crossed over her chest.

'Please explain the process, Jake?' said Linda.

Jake explained in detail the process he and Anhton had

used to extrapolate the path of the spiral and its estimated final point.

'Really, Linda, even your own people can't pinpoint the exact place of the last event.'

'Surely you can understand the countdown built into the previous events. They all lead to November 18.'

'Without concrete proof, there is nothing I will do,' said Danika. 'I have work to do. Don't contact me unless you have 100% proof of a time and place.'

Danika turned from the Glass room and left the building.

'You'd better be right about tonight, North,' snapped Linda. 'I want results. I've cancelled all leave and I have everyone on roster around the area.' Linda strode to her office and the whole floor shook when she slammed her office door closed.

'What was all that about?' asked David.

'When I came back from lunch, I heard the exchange between Linda and the President-elect,' explained Jake. 'I was staying hidden so I didn't have to go through what I just went through.' Jake turned. 'I'm going down to see Gabby. Maybe she can pluck a fingerprint out of thin air.'

7.2

After the events at lunchtime, Linda was with David at her favourite cafe in Williamstown trying to calm down.

'I don't blame anyone, David. It was just a frustrating meeting when I couldn't even convince Danika of what we knew,' said Linda.

'I think Jake took it personally though,' said David.

'I should talk to him.'

'He's a good kid and he's smart. He'll figure it out.'

'Is he still at the office?' asked Linda.

'It can wait until tomorrow. I think he's getting ready for night shift. You have us doing all sorts of odd things tonight.'

'Yeah, I kinda have.'

'Speaking of which, I have the midnight shift. I'm gonna head home and catch a few zzzz's before I watch the dark of night.' David rose and left.

Linda finished her coffee, paid and stepped outside of the cafe. She looked up and down the street and decided the direction she would start walking.

Jake was coming out of the gym when his phone began to ring. He picked it up to see that he had three other issued calls, all from Linda. 'What's up, Linda?'

'Can you meet me at my location in Williamstown?' she said. 'I saw Jeremy again today, but I don't think he saw me. I called out, but he didn't respond. I tried to follow him but lost him when he went into a house. It's been over half an hour and I can't see any movement or lights on in the house.'

'Perhaps what's happening isn't near the front of the house?' said Jake.

'I've checked. Can you meet me anyway, I don't feel easy about this?'

'Sure. I'll be there as soon as I can. Let me get your position.' Jake looked at his mini tablet and located Linda's signal. 'Got you. Wait for me.'

'I'm going to head back towards the centre of town. I first saw him come out of a warehouse. I want to see if I can get a look at it.'

Jake showered quickly and drove into Williamstown. By the time he got there, Linda had moved. He parked his new AV, grabbed a torch and walked to where Linda was. Being eight-thirty at night, it was now dark and the cloud cover wasn't helping. He stopped to check his mini tablet to see that Linda was moving quickly away from him. He started to jog and every minute or so checked his position.

'What's going on, Linda?' he asked when he called her.

'I've lost Jeremy completely, but, I saw someone dressed in black moving about suspiciously. I'm following them but I think they know, they're moving all over the place,' said Linda. 'Gotta go, they're moving again.'

Jake saw Linda's blip move again on his tablet. He turned a corner and began to go in a different direction to try and meet her from her other side rather than follow her. He soon realised they were in the old warehouse district of Williamstown. Most had been converted to apartments. Some had been converted to storage facilities. There were still a couple that seemed to be used as warehouses though. Jake slowed his progress, checked his tablet and moved cautiously from street to street and alley to alley.

'What is it, Linda?' Jake said, answering his phone.

'I think he's moving towards the dock area.'

'Are you sure it's a male?'

'I don't have time to argue about that now. The figure is not moving like a female, I know that much.'

'Okay. I'll head towards the docks and try and put him between us.'

7.3

'Jake, he ran down the alley. I'm giving chase,' Linda yelled as she chased a figure in black.

'Ok. I'm tracking you,' replied Jake. 'I'll try and circle around and cut them off.'

Left, then right at the main road, onwards for about one hundred metres then right again. Jake pushed his mini tablet into his pocket and took off at pace. He paused and checked his mini tablet. Come on, come on! Okay, I'll need to turn right down the second alley. He replaced the tablet, ran to the alley, turned into it and drew his gun.

Linda, whilst not the fittest in DFIS, was able to keep her target in sight. She had a knack for knowing which way to turn in a crisis, which she'd used on many occasions when in the field with her army unit. As she adjusted to the darkened alley, she just made out her target standing in front of a solid brick wall, pressing some information into a hand-held device.

She approached quickly, gun drawn.

'Stop what you're doing and put your hands in the air,' called Linda.

The figure looked at her and sped off down the alley. Linda fired but the figure was criss-crossing so much that she missed each time, he darted around a corner to the right and when Linda turned the same corner, he was gone. She cautiously stepped into the alley, one step at a time. Linda moved along the fence that was bordering the opposite side of the alley. One hand shining a torch along the alley in front of her, the other holding her gun firm.

Turning sharply to the far end, the edge or her torch beam caught a shadow. With the light bobbing around, she ran towards the shadow. She didn't see the obstacle in her path until it was too late. Tumbling over, her hands let go of both gun and torch. They clattered along the concrete alley.

'Aaarrrggghhh,' cried Linda, clutching at the ankle she clearly heard crack. 'JAKE!' she yelled. 'JAKE, I've broken my ank...' She couldn't finish her call for help. Her mouth was clamped firmly shut. Struggling, she was lifted and half carried, half dragged back around the corner.

She found herself staring at a blank wall when suddenly it opened. No sounds. No gears. No shushing of air escaping. Seconds later it was black. She couldn't see a thing. The dragging started again. The pain in her ankle intensified as she automatically tried to correct her position, only to falter on her broken ankle.

Jake turned into the alley where he thought he heard Linda's voice come from, but when he arrived, there was no one there. He saw her gun and torch lying on the ground but left them there. He quickly radioed for back up and gave his position. He then crept along the alley and turned the corner that Linda had come around minutes before.

Before he knew what to do, he was rushed by a black shadow and knocked to his feet. He quickly got up, saw where the shadow was fleeing and gave chase. Due to his stringent fitness routine, he was able to keep up and began to gain. He chased the shadow round corners, down alleys and even through a park, which he'd never known existed.

At one stage, he thought he'd lost his target in the back alleys of Williamstown. He stopped, consulted his tablet and lightly jogged back to the alley where Linda's gun and torch were. As he turned into the alley, he saw the shadow again. Once more, he gave chase. This time he caught the person and tackled them to the ground.

They were almost as strong as each other, and the tussle was evenly matched. Each was as determined as the other to prevail. However, in a quick move, Jake found himself being hurled into the wall of the building. Winded, he still managed to fend off the ensuing blows.

Kicking his leg in a roundhouse motion, he knocked the person off-balance. This gave Jake enough time to stand and attack. The figure he fought was just as quick and dashed off down the alley and into the next street. Jake caught up to him once again and as they tackled each other, they landed in the front garden of a local house. This drew the attention of the resident who turned on the front light, blinding Jake. In his daze, Jake was struck on the head causing him to collapse onto ground.

'What's going on out here,' called the homeowner.

The figure darted off, but Jake was unable to get to his feet and collapsed unconscious onto ground with the homeowner standing over him.

A few minutes later, Jake roused. He felt a cool cloth on his head and all sorts of other things being attached to him. He made out the flashing lights of an ambulance. The first voice he recognised was David's

'Are you alright, Jake?' he asked.

'If you call a killer headache alright, then I'm doing absolutely fine,' replied Jake.

'He's okay.' David laughed.

'Linda? Where's Linda?' asked Jake.

'She's not here.'

'No, of course she's not, that person has her. I'm sure it's a man we're dealing with now, there's no way a woman could fight like that.'

'Watchyaself, matey,' said a strong Scottish-accented female voice.

'No offence meant, Gabby,' said Jake. 'Not even you could fight like that.

'None taken, hon,' said Gabby.

'This man knew what he was doing. He was trained, and I mean trained.'

Jake sat up, but his head hurt. The paramedics tried to make him lie back down, but he refused. 'David, here, on my tablet, this is where I last saw Linda's gun and torch. She must be near there somewhere. Find her, please?'

'We'll get on to it right away. Everyone's here,' said David.

Jake, feeling reassured, lay back down and allowed the paramedics to put him in the back of the ambulance.

* * * * *

Almost delirious with pain, Linda stood herself against the wall where she was brutally tossed. In the dark, she felt her way around but couldn't feel any form of a door. She turned when the wall opened and a figure stumbled into the room. She rushed at the figure, only to be fended off by a strong arm. Gaining her footing again, she felt an arm around her throat, which dragged her along the floor. She only knew another wall had opened when she passed through it. Dragged along a dimly lit hall, this time she knew what she heard. The sounds of an elevator.

She was crudely pushed into the lift and she took the chance to gulp down huge breaths her lungs now craved. To make sure she complied, the figure pressed his foot against her broken one. Enough for her to yelp but also to let her know that if she tried anything, it would be pressed harder. This allowed the figure to gain his breath too.

'I see Jake got you then,' Linda said.

Her ankle was pressed, but she didn't cry out this time.

The lift stopped and Linda was grabbed by the arm and forcibly dragged out.

'What are you going to do with me?' asked Linda.

Silence.

Linda faltered and went over on her ankle. She screamed in pain. Crumpled on the ground, her head was pulled up roughly by her hair. She watched as the figure removed its night vision goggles. Linda looked at the eyes and gasped.

'I know those eyes,' she said. She opened her mouth to say something else but her head was snapped sharply to the left and her lifeless body was dropped to the ground.

After her body was placed into a barrel with the green liquid poured over it, it was moved to the press and left to stew. Going to a cabinet near the cot, the figure swallowed two pills and laid down to rest.

With several hours of rest, the figure rose, stretched gingerly and checked on the barrel with Linda's body in it. Satisfied with the progress, a heavy plate was placed on top of the mixture and the press engaged. When complete, the barrel was sealed and rolled next to the smaller of the two matte-black utes in the basement.

In the far left corner, a door opened and closed.

7.4

'David, here, on my tablet, this is where I last saw Linda's gun and torch. She must be near there somewhere. Find her, please?'

'We'll get on to it right away. Everyone's here,' said David.

Jake lay back down and allowed the paramedics to put him in the back of the ambulance.

David watched as the ambulance drove away. With Jake's tablet in his hand, he noted that the position Jake talked about wasn't that far. 'Gabby, Amy, you're with me. We have to find out what happened to Linda,' he said urgently.

David and Gabby walked the path to the alley, while Amy drove the forensics van behind. They turned into the alley, torches on full. They stopped and scanned up and down before entering.

'I can see the gun,' said Gabby. 'It's about halfway down.' She turned to Amy, who was just getting out of the van. 'Can you grab my kit please, Amy?'

Amy walked back a few minutes later and handed Gabby her kit with her own in the other hand.

'I want every square millimetre of this alley searched, tagged, photographed and printed. I want these walls dusted as well. If anything happened in this alley, I want to know about it,' said David, earnestly. 'One of our own is missing and another injured.' David walked to the van, grabbed a kit and began his own search from the far end of the alley.

'David,' called Gabby, 'I have the gun and torch.'

'Anything else?'

'No, but I'm sure Jake'll work it out,' said Gabby. 'He seems to have a handle on this case.'

David narrowed his eyes as he turned towards Gabby.

'Oh, sorry David,' said Gabby, looking away. 'So far, he seems to have worked out most of the connections.'

David continued to look at her. David was becoming more and more frustrated talking to Gabby.

'Well, he has. That's what's going around the office any-way.'

'I see,' he said. 'Can you finish up here?'

'Sure thing,' said Gabby. 'I'll have the data on desk by the end of the day.'

'Good, I look forward to seeing it by lunchtime. I'm going to the hospital to see how Jake's doing.'

David walked back past the van, threw his kit inside, slammed the door shut and walked to his car.

Gabby looked over her shoulder at the van.

Jake was still in emergency when David arrived.

'How's it going, Jake?'

'Sore,' replied Jake. 'Have you found Linda?'

'Not yet. I left Gabby and Amy going over the alley. If there's anything there they'll find it.'

'I want to get back to that alley as soon as I can.' Jake tried to move.

'I'm just going to have to make sure they don't let you out for a while,' said David. 'You're in no position to do any investigative work at the moment.'

'I have to find her,' insisted Jake.

'No, you don't. We can do that.'

Jake tried to move again, only to fall back in pain.

'See, you've collapsed and you hurt. You will stay away from the office for as long as you need to.'

'I was only hit on the head. I don't have any broken bones. What if I only stayed at the office and worked and let others do the foot work?'

'No, Jake. I'm the boss now and you will stay here until the you are released.'

Jake sighed heavily.

'We'll find her, Jake.'

At that moment, the doctor walked in to see Jake.

'I'm sorry, I didn't know someone was here to see you already,' she said.

'I'm his superior officer, 2ndLt David Castle, DFIS.'

'DFIS?'

'Defence Force Investigative Service. Crpl Jake North is one of my investigators,' said David.

The doctor nodded.

'How soon can I go back to work, doctor?' asked Jake. 'I have to find someone who's gone missing.'

'You're not going back to work that soon, I'm afraid,' said the doctor. 'The X-rays show no broken bones or swelling. It's a mild concussion and we're going to keep you overnight for observation.'

'What did I say, Jake.'

'None of that, actually,' said Jake.

'Enough, Jake!' said David. 'If you're back at work before Monday, provided you've been released, I will personally bundle you up and take you home. Do I make myself clear?'

'Yes, sir,' said Jake. He turned to the doctor. 'When can I go home then, doctor? How long before I'll be allowed to go back to work?'

'That depends on how well you recover,' said the doctor. 'You're a fit man and I suspect it won't be that long. We'll see how you are in the morning. I'll get you moved as soon as we can. Also, what your boss said.'

'Thank you, doctor. I'd better get going, Jake,' said David. 'I'm glad to hear you're okay. We'll find Linda. We all want to find Linda. When you're out, I'll make sure you see the forensics as soon as possible.'

David returned to his desk at DFIS HQ to find Gabby's preliminary report in his email. He smiled and sat down to read it. When he'd finished, he went down to see her.

'If you call that a preliminary report, I'd hate to see what's in the full report,' said David, as he walked into the forensics lab.

'I want to find Linda as much as anyone,' replied Gabby. 'Amy and I put everything else aside and processed our butts off to give you that prelim.'

'Don't get me wrong, I'm impressed. Is there much more that you can add?'

'Some of the tests take a little longer and we're having trouble tracing a few prints. We only have partials and the database is running through everything we have access to. So far, no results.'

'Thanks. I'll take another wander along the alley to see what else may be there.'

'How's Jake?'

'He's doing well,' said David. 'They're keeping him in overnight for observation. If he's okay, he'll be allowed home tomorrow.'

'You know he'll try and come into the office,' said Gabby.

'I told him in no uncertain terms that he is not to come into the office before Monday,' said David. 'Otherwise I said I'd personally bundle him up and take him home.'

'You're brave,' said Gabby. 'He may be shorter, but he is very fit.'

'I'm just hoping he listens this time.'

Gabby laughed. 'Let Anhton deal with him. Give him some time off as well. If Jake is desperate to do something, then Anhton can take it home for him. No matter when he sees the data, he'll figure it out.'

'I know. He's a bright kid. If anyone will crack this case, it'll be him,' said David. 'If he's right, we only have six weeks and it'll be all over.'

Gabby turned sharply. 'What will?'

'This case.'

'What's he worked out?'

'So far, he and Anhton have managed to determine that the events are a countdown and the final event will take place on November 18.'

'That's Independence Day!'

'Yes, it is,' said David. 'We've quietly alerted all relevant government departments, but we don't know what, where or how it will happen.'

'You think Jake will work it out?' asked Gabby.

'I hope so. With the bump on the head, I just hope there aren't any setbacks. With me having to take over at DFIS, he'll be pretty much on his own.'

'He'll need to have Anhton back permanently again,' said Gabby.

'Yes, he will.'

The following Monday, Jake walked into the office and to his desk. He received good wishes from all he met as he walked through the office. He dropped his satchel on the desk, retrieved his tablet and went to Lassie.

Tapping the start button on the near right corner, he watched as Lassie loaded her programs.

'Can you bring up the countdown case please? Vertical screen only.'

'One moment.'

Jake pulled a seat to the edge of the glass table and watched as the various data files flashed onto the vertical screen. He tapped a few keys on his tablet, only to discover that the file from the most recent event had already been loaded. He smiled and placed his tablet on the table.

'All done, Jake,' said Lassie.

Pondering the screen, Jake was oblivious to the company he had behind him.

'Good morning, Jake.'

Jake noticeably jumped in his chair. He stood to attention, when he saw whom it was. A man in military uniform approached, heavy badges shone on his chest.

'At ease, soldier,' said the man.

Jake relaxed. 'Why are you here, sir?'

'When we heard that your LCmdr was missing, they sent me over to look after things,' said the man. 'I know David was thinking he'd be looking after DFIS, however, it was decided to keep him on the floor to help with the investigations.'

'Does he know yet?' asked Jake.

'Does who know what?' said David as he entered, not realising they had a guest.

David stood to attention when he noticed the new arrival. 'Cmdr Dugald, how can I help you?'

'Relax, 2ndLt,' said Cmdr Peter Dugald. 'I've been sent in to watch over DFIS. I hear you've been losing some old colleagues of mine?'

'Not us personally, but we haven't located any bodies as

yet,' replied David.

'I was just about to get an update from North when you arrived,' said Peter. 'Have you discovered anything new?'

'Only more hypotheses.'

'Go on,' said Peter.

'Do you mind if I sit?' asked Jake.

Peter indicated his chair and grabbed one of his own. David remained standing.

'Well, I think we startled the perp last week,' explained Jake. 'I don't think he did what he was intending to do that night.'

'What do you mean?' said Peter.

'Even though Linda still hasn't been found, I really don't think she was the target.'

'That's a positive, I guess. What was the target?'

'I don't know. There really isn't anything specific to the previous events.'

'I don't understand.'

'Each location hasn't been specific, merely a means to an end for what was obtained, except for Linda. I surmise that it's not an organisation that's being targeted.'

'Yet you indicated a while ago that Independence Day is a target, so that would imply a government target? I've been seeing reports.'

'What I mean is that not all the stolen items have come from a location owned or controlled by any one part of society. Uhm, they haven't all been military, civilian, or government. The targets have been hit for the items they held.'

'Okay, I think I get it.'

Jake sat in thought for a moment. 'Ah. The D6 was the first item targeted. Then it was blasting caps. Then it was blasting leads. Next were the key cards and codes, followed by the electronic timer, and then the car.'

'Which is why it's been suggested that a bomb is being constructed?'

'Yes.'

'So, what was in Williamstown that might've been used for making a bomb?'

'Lassie, can you pull up a detailed schematic of all businesses within a five-kilometre radius of this location?' said Jake.

'One moment please, Jake. This will take a few minutes.'

'Thanks, Lassie,' said Jake. He turned to Peter. 'While that's computing, would you like a coffee, sir?'

'Thanks, that'd be great.'

'I'll get them,' said David.

When David returned with the coffee, Jake was looking at the screen and with the aid of a pointer, was studying the businesses in the area.

'What do you have so far?' asked David.

'I've only just begun, but so far, nothing that would tie in with the construction of a bomb,' replied Jake. 'Lassie, with the items specifically found so far, can you extrapolate what else might be needed to construct a bomb?

'I think I can do that, but it will take time.'

'Understood. Once you have that extrapolation, eliminate all business in the previous search that do not sell or manufacture any of the items required.'

'Acknowledged, Jake. I will send a message to your tablet when this is complete.'

'Why don't you come to my office, Jake, while Lassie does her job.'

Jake followed Peter but paused as he was about to enter the office.

'Are you okay, Jake?' asked Peter.

'This is, was, is, I don't know, Linda's office.'

'Ah yes, Linda,' said Peter. 'Come in and sit all the same.'

Jake tentatively sat in a chair opposite to Peter.

'I know this is hard to see someone in this chair that you've not had here before. It's no different to Linda being replaced if she was promoted or retired.'

'She's neither of those, so it is hard to see someone else in her chair.'

'No she isn't, Jake, but I have been sent here to oversee the department until Linda returns or an official replacement is appointed. In fact, I asked to come here as soon as I knew she was reported missing. I'm part of the same army unit as her and with only five of us left now, I want to make sure we stay alive.'

Jake lowered his head. 'I'm sorry, sir, for being disrespectful just now.'

'I understand, Jake. I'm here to help, not hinder. I want to resolve this as much as you do. I want you to be free to do your work the way you want using the people you want.'

'Thank you, sir,' said Jake.'

'How are you feeling after last week?'

'I'm doing quite well. The headaches have gone and I'm sleeping better each night.'

Peter shuffled some papers around on the desk, picked up a file and opened it. 'What can you tell me about Det. Anhton Roberts? How do you know him?'

Jake spat his coffee out at Peter's question.

'Ah, I see,' said Peter. 'Feel free to speak your mind.'

'Anhton, I mean Det. Roberts, has been working with us most of the year on this investigation. Initially he was the police liaison but it slowly morphed into him becoming part of the team.'

'Anything else I should know?'

'He's my partner.'

'I met him briefly this morning. He was leaving as I was arriving,' said Peter. 'He was quite happy, so we got chatting. He said he'd been looking after you all weekend.'

'Yes he did,' said Jake, looking down at his coffee.

'There's nothing to be ashamed of, Jake, he's a nice guy. You should be lucky to have him. Did you know he wants to join DFIS? He told me and then I saw his application on Linda's desk.'

'He's not said anything to me.'

'Perhaps he wanted it to be a surprise. I'm still in two minds about couples working in the same department together. Makes it hard to separate work life from home life.'

'So why are you telling me?'

'I've noticed how happy he was and then your reaction when I mentioned his name. Your eyes lit up. It was noticeable.'

Jake nodded. 'Lassie's finished,' said Jake, as his phone vibrated on the chair beside him.

'Let's go have a look,' said Peter.

Jake walked quickly to Lassie to see the results. Peter followed him and they both looked intently at the vertical screen. Only six businesses now showed. Two of them were eliminated immediately as they were electronics companies. Another because they handled blasting leads and caps. The remaining three handled components that could be used to make bombs, but the only product of interest to Jake was electrical wire, which could be used to transmit the signal from the timer to the blasting leads via a joiner box.

'Call them and see if they've had any problems lately,' said Peter, leaving the room. 'Keep me informed.'

'I will, sir,' said Jake.

Jake went back to his desk and rang the companies to discover that there had been no break-ins recently and each agreed to keep DFIS informed if any such event took place.

After making himself a coffee, he went back to Lassie. Sitting on the chair, he stared at the screen.

'Lassie, can you bring up the projection for the arc of the spiral, please?'

'One moment.'

Jake watched as the map of Melbourne appeared. Each completed section of the spiral now a solid line, there was the broad arc that covered the next possible target.

'Thank you, Lassie. Please enlarge the proposed next arc and magnify to full screen.'

'One moment.'

'Whatya doin', gayboy?' said Gabby as she entered the room.

'Checking over the next event.'

'When is the next proposed event, Jake?' asked Gabby.

'A week from Wednesday, which will be two weeks from the previous one. Then the big one is only a week after that.'

'Do we have any indication of where it might take place?

'I've had Lassie calculate a possible area,' said Jake. 'The next event is going to be somewhere in the broad vicinity of the University of Melbourne.'

'Why target a Uni?'

'The Uni itself may not be the target. I was using that as a reference to give us an idea of the locale.'

'What else is in the area?' asked Gabby.

'Here's the northern end of the Uni. I'm gonna use that as a nominal central point,' said Jake.

'I think we can rule out the Zoo,' said Gabby.

'Unless the perp has discovered a way of using copious amounts of animal waste as part of the bomb.'

'That'd be a stinker if he did.'

Jake groaned. 'The hospitals are there, and there's the...' Jake pressed a few more buttons on Lassie and as able to access CCTV of the area around the building. He froze and reached for the phone on the wall. 'Peter, I mean, sir, can you come to Lassie please. Bring David as well if you see him.' He hung up the phone.

Peter and David entered the room. They greeted Gabby, who stepped into the background.

'What is it, Jake?' said Peter.

'I was going over the potential impact zone for the next event, as you can see here,' said Jake, indicating the magnified section of the north of Melbourne around the university. 'I used the northern end of the university as a nominal central point. Then we began looking at what was around.'

'I think we can rule out the Zoo,' said Peter.

'We did that already. I then looked around further and came across this building.' Jake re-opened the CCTV window of the building.

'This is not good,' said Peter. He pulled his phone from his pocket and rapidly dialled a number. 'Dawn, it's Peter ... yeah, I'm well. You? ... Good. I'm here at DFIS temporarily until they locate Linda. I've been going over the information about the case. Hey, what's the address of your temporary office? ... It is ... no, no problem at this stage, but I'll let you know soon. Bye.' Peter moved around to the vertical screen and manually enlarged an area on the west side of Royal Pde towards the zoo.

'What is that building?' asked Jake. 'Why are there guards moving about an old office building?'

'It used to be an old office building until it was recently acquired by the new government to house the PSU.'

'Who, or what, is the PSU?' said Jake.

'The Presidential Security Unit.'

7.5

Jake lay back in Anhton's arms and all[owed the bub]bles of his spa to soothe and relax his body. Sinc[e ...]ter with the alleged perp, he'd been finding ba[th ...] comfort. With a drink by his side and his favou[rite ...] playing softly in the background, Jake began to po[nder the] fight and the disappearance of Linda.

The darkened figure was very well trained, al[so] seemed military. None of the houses nearby have see[n or] heard of Linda, so she must be in the vicinity of the build[ing.] must investigate further. Nothing stolen that night, as m[ight] be presumed, but wiring companies are located in the are[a] around HQ. Wiring potentially needed to make a fuller con- nection for a bomb. Soldiers and civilians missing, most of the people missing belonged to the same army unit, now dis- banded with most also discharged. Enough materials collect- ed, allegedly stolen but not proven, to make a bomb - but how will it be delivered and where? Diplomatic Forden AV stolen, along with a set of Forden key cards and activation codes...

Jake sat up suddenly, reached for his tablet, and m[ade] some notes.

'What's the matter?' asked Anhton.

'Just need to make some notes before I forge[t,' said] Jake.

Resuming his relaxation, he nestled back int[o ...] arms and allowed the care being given to wash ov[er ...]

'That'd be a stinker if he did.'

Jake groaned. 'The hospitals are there, and there's the...' Jake pressed a few more buttons on Lassie and as able to access CCTV of the area around the building. He froze and reached for the phone on the wall. 'Peter, I mean, sir, can you come to Lassie please. Bring David as well if you see him.' He hung up the phone.

Peter and David entered the room. They greeted Gabby, who stepped into the background.

'What is it, Jake?' said Peter.

'I was going over the potential impact zone for the next event, as you can see here,' said Jake, indicating the magnified section of the north of Melbourne around the university. 'I used the northern end of the university as a nominal central point. Then we began looking at what was around.'

'I think we can rule out the Zoo,' said Peter.

'We did that already. I then looked around further and came across this building.' Jake re-opened the CCTV window of the building.

'This is not good,' said Peter. He pulled his phone from his pocket and rapidly dialled a number. 'Dawn, it's Peter ... yeah, I'm well. You? ... Good. I'm here at DFIS temporarily until they locate Linda. I've been going over the information about the case. Hey, what's the address of your temporary office? ... It is ... no, no problem at this stage, but I'll let you know soon. Bye.' Peter moved around to the vertical screen and manually enlarged an area on the west side of Royal Pde towards the zoo.

'What is that building?' asked Jake. 'Why are there guards moving about an old office building?'

'It used to be an old office building until it was recently acquired by the new government to house the PSU.'

'Who, or what, is the PSU?' said Jake.

'The Presidential Security Unit.'

7·5

Jake lay back in Anhton's arms and allowed the bubbles of his spa to soothe and relax his body. Since the encounter with the alleged perp, he'd been finding baths a great comfort. With a drink by his side and his favourite music playing softly in the background, Jake began to ponder the fight and the disappearance of Linda.

The darkened figure was very well trained, almost seemed military. None of the houses nearby have seen or heard of Linda, so she must be in the vicinity of the building, must investigate further. Nothing stolen that night, as might be presumed, but wiring companies are located in the area around HQ. Wiring potentially needed to make a fuller connection for a bomb. Soldiers and civilians missing, most of the people missing belonged to the same army unit, now disbanded with most also discharged. Enough materials collected, allegedly stolen but not proven, to make a bomb - but how will it be delivered and where? Diplomatic Forden AV stolen, along with a set of Forden key cards and activation codes...

Jake sat up suddenly, reached for his tablet, and made some notes.

'What's the matter?' asked Anhton.

'Just need to make some notes before I forget,' said Jake.

Resuming his relaxation, he nestled back into Anhton's arms and allowed the care being given to wash over him.

8.1

A lone figure trotted lightly along the semi-darkened street. The small matte-black utility was parked where it could be most hidden from the streetlights. Stopping opposite a rear parking entry, the figure stopped and dropped to the ground. Removing his backpack, he checked its contents and nodded once. The figure watched a guard appear across the road at the entrance to the parking garage. The guard walked to the street, looked up and down and then returned inside. At that moment, the figure dashed across the road and slipped into a darkened corner of the parking garage. Making negligible noise, the figure squatted in the dark and removed his backpack. As he did, he touched a metal pipe that sent a small echo through the near empty garage.

The guard turned and peered along the length of the garage. In the far corner, he saw the figure squatting.

'Stop!'

The figure remained silent.

The guard approached, his gun at the ready in his hand.

'What are you doing down here? This is private proper-ty,' said the guard.

The figure looked down and reached into the backpack. The guard froze and watched as the figure placed what looked like a rifle against its shoulder. The guard didn't know it had been fired until he felt a stab of pain and looked down to see a dart sticking out of his chest. He pulled it out, looked at the dart oddly, wavered slightly then collapsed to the ground.

The figure raced over to the guard, found no pulse, dragged the guard across the ground, pushed the body be-hind the only car in the garage, and proceeded with its mis-sion. Quickly dashing from pillar to pillar, the figure attached small black packages to the desired locations. Walking quick-ly to the garage entrance, the figure removed a small device from the backpack, pressed a series of buttons and watched as lights flickered on each of the packages.

Placing the backpack on its back, the figure trotted back to the utility. Sitting in the cabin, the figure retrieved the small device once more. Accessing another icon, he en-tered a series of characters. As the ute drove away, a series of explosions rocked the relatively quiet area.

8.2

The late evening news was just beginning so Dawn Forde got up to make a fresh cup of coffee. She glanced at her watch and looked towards the front door. She returned to the couch and was startled to see a live cross to a burning building.

'We're live now at the offices of the Presidential Security Unit. All we could ascertain from residents was that they heard a series of explosions coming from the basement car park. Police are not saying anything at this stage until the scene can be properly investigated. The explosives used have been so powerful that neighbouring houses have been damaged. Residents nearby say that they saw lights earlier in the evening but could not be sure if anyone was inside the building at the time. No one from the Presidential Security Unit is willing to speak with us at this time. We know that there are still people who are against the independence of Victoria and Tasmania. This could be another attempt at trying to derail a major change in the history of our two great states. I'll have more as soon as we have the information. Back to the studio.'

Dawn sat back and simply stared at the TV. She jumped when she heard the front door open.

Jeremy came in, looking a bit dishevelled, but that was pushed aside when he saw the look on Dawn's face. 'What's the matter, Dawn?'

'The offices have been destroyed.'

'Which ones?'

'Our old ones,' said Dawn.

'What do you mean old ones?'

'The offices we used to be in for the PSU.'

'Aren't you in Parkville?' asked Jeremy.

'No,' said Dawn. 'We had to do a rush relocate.'

'Where are you now?'

'We're not allowed to say at this stage,' said Dawn. 'I'm sorry, but I'm not even allowed to tell you.'

'You look terrible. Come and give me a hug,' said Jeremy.

'Thank you, baby. I need one.' Dawn allowed Jeremy's large arms to envelop and hold her. Jeremy stood and stared at the TV screen, which was showing a brief rundown on the bombing of the offices.

8.3

Jake and Anhton parked their car and walked over to the first officer they saw. After speaking with him for several minutes, they crossed the line and approached the smouldering building. Fire officers were everywhere and one stopped Jake and Anhton before they got too close.

'We haven't been able to secure the whole building, Cpl, I strongly suggest you don't go inside,' said the fire officer.

'Do we know if anyone was in the building yet?' asked Jake.

'As far as we can tell, the building was empty, although the security company hasn't heard from its guard on duty since about ten thirty tonight.'

'When did the explosions happen?'

'From what we've been told, they happened about ten thirty,' said the fire officer.

'Anhton, see what you can find out. Call forensics while you're at it.'

'Yes, sir,' said Anhton.

Anthon moved carefully around the rubble at the rear of the building. He approached the main door and walked carefully towards it. He stopped when he saw what was hanging from the handle. He walked back to Jake.

'I've found some more items, Jake,' said Anhton.

'Where? What have you seen?' said Jake.

Anhton led Jake to the front door.

'Here, on the main doors. A clock face, showing the time as ten to one, along with the three of spades.'

'We'll get Gabby to deal with those when she gets here.

Jake and Anhton were leaning against Jake's car when DFIS forensics arrived. Gabby hopped out of one side of the van whilst David hopped out of the other.

'Show Gabby what you found, Anhton,' said Jake. 'I'm gonna see if we can get inside at all.'

'This way, Gabby,' said Anhton.

As soon as Gabby was set up, she had tagged and bagged the clock face and the card. She had also fingerprinted the door.

'What do you think, Gabby?' asked Anhton.

'I'm not sure yet. If these belong to same group as the rest of the year, then there shouldn't be any fingerprints or marks on either of these,' said Gabby.

'What about the card?'

'Looking at it inside the plastic bag, I can see the hole in the lower left corner, so it'll probably match up with the ones we already have. So, no joy there.'

'We can only hope,' said Anhton.

Jake went over to the fire chief to check on the state of the building.

'Crpl Jake North, DFIS,' said Jake, offering his hand. The fire chief accepted. 'Is the building stable enough for us to have a look inside?'

'We've just finished a preliminary check and it seems stable enough at the front, but I'd prefer to keep the rear off limits though.'

'Understandable. What if one of your men accompanied one of forensics analysts as they look for evidence?'

'Do you guys have safety gear in that van of yours?'

'I think we do,' said Jake.

'Good. Anyone going near the rear of the building will need to be wearing at least a hard hat, more if you have it.'

'Got it.'

Jake looked for Gabby, who was busy bagging and tagging the items at the front door.

'Hey Gab, do we have hard hats and safety vests in our vans?' asked Jake.

'Sure. Sometimes we need them. Why, what's up?'

'If one of the fireys accompanies us, the rear of the building can be checked. Can you stay here and handle the front? I'll take David.'

'Sounds good to me,' said Gabby.

Jake found David and explained what was happening. Soon Jake and David had geared up and had been teamed with a firey to have a look inside the basement carpark.

'What about me?' asked Anhton.

'You'll just have to wait for us to finish,' said David. 'Let's roll, Jakey-boy.'

They walked towards the entrance to the car park and walked down the slope. The firey was a head of them, his torch bright and clear. Jake and David activated theirs and soon they were inside.

'Jake, I want you to tag and bag anything you see that looks out of the ordinary,' said David.

'We should probably have Gabby down here too,' suggested Jake.

'It would be good, but I need the front door done.' David surveyed the situation. 'Start at the back wall where the damage seems greatest.'

'Got it.'

'I'll start at this end and meet you in the middle.'

Jake and David got to work and began to carefully work their way around the edges of the rubble, trying to determine the origin of the blast. Items were bagged and tagged as they went, but a lot were indiscernible. Jake climbed over the rubble and found his way further in.

'Gabby, can you hear me?' he yelled.

'Yes, sweetie, I can.'

'Good. I'm taking some photographs of shrapnel spatter on the back of the garage and ...' he broke off.

'What? What is it, Jake? Are you ok?'

As Jake looked around and took photographs, he stopped when his light fell upon a large red splatter on one wall. He moved closer and found the cause of the splatter.

'Yes, I'm fine. I've found the remains of a car down here in the far corner and there's a smooshed body on the wall behind it. Smooshed only because the car has been blown against the wall. You'd better get a body bag down here. This may be the guard that hasn't been accounted for yet.'

'Right on it,' said Gabby.

Several minutes later, Jake turned to see Gabby scrambling over the rubble to get to him.

'You got pics?' asked Gabby.

'Yes I do,' said Jake.

'I think a large bucket would've been better than a body bag.'

Gabby lay the bag on the ground and began to transport the various pieces of the body from its position behind the car to the bag.

'I doubt we'll be able to carry it out the way we came in without moving some of the rubble. We might tear a hole in the bag,' said Gabby. 'We also need to move the car.'

'We need to find another way out,' said Jake.

Jake looked around and found a door, but a large amount of rubble blocked it from opening.

'David, we have a door down here, it probably leads up to the lobby, but rubble is blocking it. We may need to use it to get the body bag out. Also I reckon we get as much of the car out,' said Jake.

'I'll go take a look,' said David.

It was several minutes before David spoke to Jake again.

'Jake, the front doors are locked,' said David. 'I've got the fireys about to break it open so we can get inside.'

'Sounds good to me,' said Jake.

Jake and Gabby looked above them as they heard the

crash of the main doors being broken down. As soon as that happened, the firey that had initially entered the carpark with David and Jake, clambered over the rubble with a colleague.

'Hi there, we heard you needed some rubble moved?'

'Glad you could make it,' said Jake.

About ten minutes later, the door was clear of rubble and David was making his way to the part of the carpark where Jake and Gabby were.

'Jake, can you give me a hand with this bumper?' said Gabby. Jake went over and helped gently pull the bumper from the dead guard's chest. The two firemen then took the bumper from Gabby and Jake. 'Carefully carry this and place it by our truck. Make sure no one moves it or touches it once you've laid it down. It's now evidence.'

They nodded and soon returned to carry more pieces out. Jake and Gabby guided the fireys to take as many parts as they could from the carpark. Once they had finished, they then helped move the remains of the car away from the wall

Gabby dragged the body bag towards the wall. 'Can you hand me the spatula please, Jake?' she asked. 'I need to remove this man from the wall.'

'Smooshed is a good word for him, Jake,' said Gabby. 'Your command of English and forensics is far beyond anything we could've said.'

'Ha, ha,' said Jake. 'I called it as I saw it.'

'Trying to keep my dinner down, folks,' called David.

'After this long, you still can't stand a little bit of a smooshed body?' said Gabby.

After an hour, the remains of the body were carried up the stairs in the bag and placed inside the van to be taken to the DFIS morgue for examination.

David, Jake, and Gabby stood in front of the doorway and looked at what was left of the parking garage.

'What could have done this much damage?' asked Gabby.

'Residents reckon they heard a few explosions,' said David.

Jake dropped to his knees and began fossicking through his kit. 'What component in a single blast could've done this much damage?'

'What are you looking for, Jake?' asked Gabby.

'Do we have a solution to test for D6?'

'We do, yes.' Gabby reached into her kit and removed a small plastic spray bottle containing a pale green liquid. 'Surely there's no way anyone would use D6 so close to the general public.'

'If this was the same person who stole the D6 back in January, then who knows what they're capable of. How do you use this stuff?' he asked, pointing at the bottle.

'You just spray where you think the substance might've been used,' explained Gabby, as she began to spray near where she was standing.

Jake retrieved the same bottle of green liquid from his kit, walked over to a pile of rubble and began to spray. Small spots of orange began to appear amongst the pale green.

'Well I'll be,' said Gabby. 'I wouldn't've thought to check for D6.'

'Then you'd better gather samples to make sure, Gabby,' said David. 'Good job, Jake. Let's get this info back to HQ and processed. We don't have much time left.'

With kits overflowing, David and Gabby got into their van and prepared to leave.

'Shit, Anhton,' said Jake. 'One moment, David.' Jake rushed over to where Anhton stood. 'Hey, sweetie,'

'Hey there, Jake,' said Anhton. 'I thought you'd guys had forgotten about me standing out here, in the cold, all alone, no one to talk to, nothing to do but wait, and wait.'

'Sorry about that,' said Jake. 'Maybe if- no, when you become part of DFIS you won't have to wait for us. Anyway, we've got quite a bit of evidence to go through. We're heading back to HQ to get it tested and analysed. All hands on deck?'

* * * * *

All morning, whenever Jake tried to poke his nose inside Gabby's lab, she'd shut him down and throw him out. He stood in front of Lassie and visually reviewed all the info he had keyed in. Suddenly a whole lot of new info began to filter into the various parts of the case file.

Jake summarised them in his mind as they flashed up;

- D6 confirmed as explosive substance;

- Body found confirmed as the guard who was missing - Jake conducted a quick cross-reference of the name but it had no matches to any of the previous unaccounted for people;

- D6 used was unauthorised - Gabby had checked the D6 usage registry.

Jake made notes appropriately that the information about the PSU being the potential target had been substantiated. With a yawn that lasted a few seconds, he had begun the shutdown procedure for Lassie, when he heard his name being called.

'Jake, are you still here?'

'Yes, sir, I am,' Jake replied.

Peter entered the Glass room with Dawn Forde.

'Excellent. I was wondering if you could show the head of the PSU where you're up to at the moment,' said Peter.

'Sure thing, Peter.'

'Pleased to meet you again, Ma'am,' said Jake.

'I believe I owe you our thanks,' said Dawn.

'Excuse me?'

'Peter tells me you forecast the area of the next attack?'

'Lassie helped me speculate where the next event might take place,' said Jake. 'It was Peter who decided it was most likely going to the PSU building.'

'I only knew because I was privy to the information and that is only because I am married to the president-elect,' said Peter. 'Otherwise I would not have known.'

'In this case, it worked out to our advantage,' said Dawn. 'Who knows what would have happened if you did not recognise the building.'

'Who'd want to attack an empty building anyway?' said Jake.

'I suspect that they didn't know it was going to be empty,' said Peter.

'Did you have people covering the building, Peter?' asked Dawn.

'We had passed on the information to the Police and of course your division, as to what they did with it, I don't know,' said Peter.

'I know we had our people watching our new premises, but we didn't think it useful to have anyone watch the old building,' said Dawn. 'I encouraged the Police to do so, but it would appear that they ignored me. How did you come to a political conclusion?'

'When we began to analyse the data from each event, we found a pattern. Extrapolating the formula, and following the pattern, we discovered a countdown. That led to November 18 as the most likely target date.'

'Independence Day?'

'That's correct,' said Jake.

'Therefore, following the political line, we presumed that the PSU building might become a target,' said Peter.

'What you're saying is that in three weeks, there may be another attack?'

Jake went quiet for a moment.

'It's ok, Jake, you can tell her the truth,' said Peter.

Jake looked up and calmed himself. 'Yes, Ma'am, I believe Independence Day is going to be the final event.'

'Thank you, Crpl. I don't like to hear it, but at least I know so I can best prepare our new President and her staff for any last minute action,' said Dawn. 'Do you have any idea how it might happen? Or even where? Let alone when in the day?'

'So far, all events have taken place at night, but that doesn't mean it won't happen at some other time that particular day.'

'Do you have any ideas at all?' asked Dawn.

Jake restarted the Glass and waited. 'Lassie here has all the data we have.'

Lassie beeped and Jake turned to the screen. 'If you look at the screen, you can see all the data we've collected so far.'

Dawn silently looked at the screen for several minutes. 'Let's see, five members of the one army unit are currently listed as missing, presumed dead?'

'Yes, Ma'am.'

'Enough materials have been stolen to make a significant bomb, some of its destructive power we saw overnight.'

'Yes, Ma'am.'

'You have no suspects at this stage?'

'That's been the toughest piece of missing information to swallow.'

Dawn turned to Peter. 'Do you know about this, Peter? You know that those five missing members of the army unit are your former colleagues?'

'Unfortunately, I do, Dawn. I trust 100% that they have examined every nook and cranny of evidence brought in. This person is very efficient and hasn't left a trace,' Peter replied with conviction.

'Fair enough. I've never come across anyone who hasn't left something behind,' said Dawn.

'Neither have we,' added Jake. 'This man is well planned, well-educated and well trained.'

'Are you sure it's a male?' asked Dawn.

'Most definitely, Dawn. I had an encounter with him a few weeks ago.'

'Right. What about the theft of the Forden?' said Dawn. 'How does that fit in.'

'I'm not sure about that, but it may be the vehicle that delivers the final device,' said Jake.

'Should we be taking all Fordens off the road until after November 18?' asked Peter.

'We can't do that, Peter,' said Dawn.

'Why not?'

'Fordens are being used to move the Presidential party to Government House for the signing of the Charter of Independence,' explained Dawn. 'We don't have enough time to order a new fleet of vehicles and have them security fitted in three weeks. It's taken months to get the fleet right as it is. That's not an option.'

'Can we restrict the use of Fordens that day?' suggested Peter. 'Perhaps put a screen around the city centre and all government buildings?'

'That's a possibility,' said Dawn.

'What about a register of authorised vehicles that will

be allowed to move within the secure precinct that day?' said Jake.

'I think that can work,' said Dawn. 'I'll get staff on to it first thing tomorrow.'

Dawn looked at the screen once more.

'I see you think there'll be another event a week before Independence Day?'

'Yes, if the pattern follows true,' said Jake.

'Do you have a suspected target yet?'

'Only a target zone,' said Jake. 'Lassie, can you bring up the predicted target zone for Event Nine.'

'One moment please, Jake.'

'This shouldn't take too long at all, Dawn,' said Jake.

'Here is the information you requested, Jake,' said Lassie.

They looked at the screen and using a red light pointer, Jake circled the target zone.

'Right, I need to make a phone call,' said Dawn. 'Thank you, Jake, you have given me a lot of very useful information. Thank you too, Peter, for letting me catch up with the latest data.'

'Thanks, Jake,' said Peter, 'We'll have a chat ourselves in the morning.'

'Yes, sir.'

Jake turned to Lassie and closed it down once more.

8.4

Jake reverse parked his SUV against the railing of the car park lookout. Glancing around, he quickly changed into some more comfortable clothes, whilst Anhton looked on.

'Why didn't you get changed at home?' asked Anhton.

'What, and look like a slob when I buy some food? I think not,' said Jake.

'Snob.'

He opened the rear of his SUV, opened the meal they purchased on their way to the lookout, sat cross-legged in the back and looked out over the city, as the sky slowly dimmed.

'I've never had fish and chips at this altitude before,' said Anhton.

'Then be quiet and eat.'

'I'll eat and you can talk.'

Taking his time, Jake didn't rush his portion of the meal and by the time he'd finished, the sun had set. With the lights twinkling below him, he calmed his mind and opened his tablet. He looked at the information from the Spiral case (as they were now calling it) and pondered the most recent events.

'This is what I have now;

- PSU attack implies a political target, even though it was the first political attack,

- November 18 is a major political event,

What if remaining target is political?'

'You're sure it's political?' asked Anhton. 'What if it's been that all along?'

'Less talk, more silence.'

'I see how it is.'

Jake made a mental note to have a look at the projected target zone for the next attack.

'So, presuming that a Forden will be used at some stage, we now have the urgency to try and find that stolen car.'

'Do you need me to hassle the police station?'

'No, we did all we could that day. I doubt we would've found anything of value even if we had been able to get to the site the day after.'

'Fair enough.'

'I do need to speak with Dawn and see if I can get a copy of the register they've created for authorised Fordens.'

Jake and Anhton also recapped the details of all the other events.

'How can someone be so clean,' said Jake, standing and stretching his legs.

'Maybe we need to go back to the alley where you had that encounter. Linda seemed to think it was significant.'

'We could also start from the position she was at when she first contacted me.'

'There's our to-do list for tomorrow morning.'

'By the way, I saw this ad the other and thought it might come in handy,' said Anhton.

'What is it?'

'It seems to be an electronic device that will allow the user to find undisclosed or hidden locks. Then by recalibrating the device, it can be used to decode those locks.'

'How did you get this information?' said Jake.

'I got an email.'

'And you opened it?'

'I'm not that stupid,' said Anhton. 'I manually typed the link to their website and it looks legitimate, although I couldn't find the device that had been advertised.'

'I don't like the sound of it at all.'

'I rang the company and the person who answered the phone didn't seem to know either but confirmed that they do send targeted emails.'

'You think the device is legit?' asked Jake.

'If it is it will come in very handy.'

'We'll see. Forward it to me later.'

Jake turned off the tablet and increased the volume of his music. Anhton, learning Jake's meditation techniques, was now sitting cross-legged on the back of the SUV. They only came out of their mediation when a security guard interrupted them, coming along to close the parking area.

9

9.1

'The traffic isn't bad for a Thursday night,' commented Anhton, as he drove home from the lookout.

Jake groaned.

'That's more than I can say about my stomach,' said Jake.

'What's wrong? Do I need to stop?' said Anhton, reaching over to place his hand on Jake's.

'Not yet but be prepared.'

'This isn't going to end well.'

Jake groaned again. 'Pull over. Quickly.'

Anhton did his best to find somewhere safe to pull over. Jake opened the door and rushed for the side of the road. Anhton winced at every sound Jake made as he vomited heavily.

After a few minutes of silence, Jake crawled back into the car.

'Baby, I need to get you to a hospital,' said Anhton. 'You're whiter than me in my footy shorts at the beach.'

Jake tried to laugh but it hurt so he groaned again.

'No, just take me home,' said Jake. 'Maybe call Peter on the way and explain what's happened, without the graphics.'

Anhton made the call and whilst Anhton did most of the talking, Jake did groan once or twice in response to a question from Peter. At least Jake knew he had until Monday before coming back to work.

They made it to the other side of town and weren't that far from home when Jake ordered the car stop again. Once more Jake was throwing up violently.

This time Jake had no choice and Anhton drove him to the hospital. Jake didn't protest.

As Anhton helped Jake into the emergency waiting room, Jake couldn't hold back and vomited again. Two nurses came to his aid as those around him moved away. Cleaners were called and as Anhton left emergency to park the car, Jake was wheeled into a treatment room.

'What have you been doing tonight?' asked the nurse attending to him. 'By the way, I'm Katie.'

'I was up at the Mount Dandenong lookout having dinner with my partner,' replied Jake.

'At the restaurant?'

'No, out of the back of the car. We bought our food at the bottom of the hill and drove up.'

'What did you eat?' asked Katie.

'We both had fish and chips.'

'Did you have anything else with yours that your partner didn't?'

Jake thought for a moment. 'I had a couple of the packets of tartare sauce included with mine and Anhton asked for lemon.'

At that moment, Anhton poked his head into the treatment room.

'You must be Anhton,' said Katie. 'I'm Katie, helping your friend.'

'Hello. How is he?' asked Anhton.

Jake began to make the noises to vomit again. Katie grabbed a bag and Anhton looked away.

'I'll go and get him something to help settle the stomach. I'll be right back,' said Katie.

'Did we throw everything away before we left the car park?' asked Jake.

'Yeah, I'm pretty sure we did,' said Anhton. 'Why?'

'I have a sneaking suspicion that the tartare sauce may have been out of date.'

'You want me to have a look in the car?'

'Do you mind?' Jake threw up again.

Anhton turned away and when the noises stopped he turned to look at Jake. 'I'll be right back.'

As Anhton left, Katie returned.

'He okay? He looked a little pale,' asked Katie.

'I don't think he likes hearing or seeing people throw up,' said Jake. 'The things you learn.'

Katie smiled. 'So back to what you ate?'

'I've asked Anhton to have a look at the back of the car to see if there happens to be a packet of tartare sauce I didn't use. I have a sneaking suspicion that it might have been out of date.'

'That would explain the vomiting,' said Katie. 'We're going to take some blood and make sure that's there's nothing else that might be causing this. Are you normally a health conscious man?'

'As much as I can.' Jake threw his head back, held his stomach and began to breathe deeply.

Katie grabbed a sick bag, but Jake waved it away as not needed. She ducked out of the cubicle and returned moments later with a cart. She began to place items into the plastic dish on top. Next she grabbed a tourniquet and wrapped it around Jake's left arm. She tapped at his arm and when she was satisfied, swabbed the skin. Jake winced at the sting and waited.

'I think I have enough,' said Katie.

'Do I have any left?' asked Jake.

'No, you're only faking being sick,' said Katie, laughing. 'Let me get this away for processing.' She left with the cart.

Anhton returned a few minutes later.

'What was the use-by date?' asked Jake.

'Dunno. We threw everything away,' said Anhton.

'Bugger. Oh well, I still think that's what's caused all this.'

Katie spied Anhton when she returned with a covered tray. 'Any luck?'

'No. we had thrown everything away,' said Anhton.

Katie placed the small tray on the trolley beside the bed and removed the cover. 'You'll have to be nice and strong now. I have to give you this injection,' said Katie, as if she was speaking to a small child. 'It's probably going to hurt, but if you're really good, I might let you have a lollipop.'

Jake smiled, as did Katie, but Anhton looked confused.

'I'll explain later, dear,' said Jake.

Katie pushed Jake's sleeve higher, swabbed a spot on his upper arm and inserted the needle.

'See, now that didn't hurt at all,' said Katie.

'What have you given him?' asked Anhton.

'Short of bringing on another bought of vomiting, I've injected him with an electrolyte rich solution along with a mild sedative. The electrolytes to replace those he's lost and a sedative to help relax his stomach. It will make him drowsy, but he'll be fine. The doctor should be around soon to check.'

At two am in the morning, the emergency department sent him home. Jake threw up once more and after they had given him a second injection to ease the cramping and vomiting in his stomach, they felt that the worst had passed.

When Jake arrived at work the Monday after the former PSU building had been attacked, he was called into Peter's office immediately.

'Morning, Jake, I trust you're feeling better today?' asked Peter.

'Yes I am, thanks, Peter,' replied Jake.

'That's good to hear. I'd like you to take the rest of the week to recover properly though.'

'With all due respect, Sir, I can't do that.'

'Why not?'

'The next event is Wednesday of next week, November 11. I'd like to find out as much as I can before that date so we can do our best to be ready, and hopefully catch whoever it is doing all this.'

'Okay, but on one condition- actually a couple. Firstly, you let David do any running around. Secondly, no dodgy fish and chips.'

Jake laughed. 'Thank you. I promise, no more fish and chips again. Period. David can do as much running around as he likes, I'll just tell him where to go.'

'That's what I like to hear,' said Peter. 'When this is over, if that ever happens, I want you to take a long holiday.'

'It will be over, and it's a deal.'

'How can you be sure it will be over?' Peter looked at Jake.

'The countdown finishes on November 18. I doubt we'll see anything else happen after that. I just want to catch whoever is doing this before that day.'

'Of course. I keep forgetting about that. I've had a lot of other things to organise lately, what with the integration of police and military, some of the details of our cases don't always get filed away correctly,' said Peter, tapping his temple. 'Go find out what's going on. I know you can work this out.'

Jake got up and left the office. Putting his satchel on his desk, he retrieved his tablet, walked over to the Glass zone, and activated Lassie. While the computer booted up, he went and got himself a cup of tea.

'Morning, Lassie,' said Jake upon his return to the Glass zone.

'Good morning, Jake. How can I be of assistance today?'

'I need a projected path of the spiral arm from the last event location continuing so that the spiral concludes in the city centre.'

'That should not be difficult at all. I will let you know when I am finished.'

'Thanks, Lassie.' Jake returned to his desk and reviewed all the data, again, on his computer screen.

He didn't get much done as he heard David arrive. 'Okay, what did you say to him?'

'Say what to whom?' asked Jake.

'Peter. He said he was going to send you home for a rest this week.'

'With all that we have to do to catch a crook, I don't think so.'

'I'd better go and have a word with him then.'

'It's all good. I get to tell you what to do and make you run around,' said Jake, trying not to laugh too much.

'Is that so?'

'Yes, that's right,' said Peter, chuckling slightly as he approached Jake's desk. 'Morning, David.'

'Morning, Peter. I see you relented.'

'He gave a good argument and promised to make you run around. How could I refuse that?' said Peter.

'Quite easily,' said David.

Jake's tablet buzzed at that moment. 'Good, Lassie's finished. Come on, David, let's go see what's happening next.'

'What did you get Lassie to do?' asked David, as he detoured to his desk to drop his satchel.

'I asked her to project a path of the spiral arm from the last event to conclude in the centre of the city,' said Jake.

'That could produce a large area to cover.'

'Possibly, which means we'll have to get it sorted out quickly.'

They walked in to the Glass Zone to see a moderately thin area of shading on the map on the screen starting from the point in Parkville where the former PSU building was attacked and arcing through Hawthorn and Richmond to finish at a nominal spot in the middle of the city of Melbourne.

'Lassie, can you isolate all businesses within that projected area please?'

'One moment.'

In a few seconds, business premises became bolder against the background.

'Now can you add commercial buildings, whether they are currently being used for commercial means or not?'

More properties were highlighted.

'This will take us weeks to sort though,' said David.

'No it won't,' said Jake. 'It's now a process of elimination.' Jake looked at his tablet. 'Ah yes, Lassie, are you able to isolate, using a different colour, any premises in the projected area that are being used for any political purpose?'

'That may take a little longer, Jake. I will need to cross reference telephone and government directories.'

'Take as long as you need, Lassie.'

'I will alert you when I am done.'

'What's with the political search?' asked David.

'Before I got sick, I was meditating at the top of Mount Dandenong and I got to thinking that if the PSU, well former PSU building, was a target, then why not others.'

'You think all these related events have a political end?'

'It's a strong possibility that can't be ruled out. Especially right now. We are going through significant political change. It stands to reason that there will be at least one person who is so violently against it that they will take whatever measures they think are right.'

'You think we are dealing with someone that is potentially unstable?'

'Actually, no I don't. I do know we are dealing with someone who is very intelligent, knows clearly and exactly what they are doing and.'

'Do you think they know we're onto them, even though we don't know who they are?'

'I'm not sure about that one,' said Jake. 'We may never know. Besides, we have to catch them first.'

'Okay, so if this is politically motivated, what, or even who, will be the next target?'

'We'll have to wait and see what Lassie discovers.'

'Yes, we will. Have you had breakfast yet?'

'Yeah, but I'm happy for you to buy me more.'

David laughed.

* * * * *

Jake and David returned about forty-five minutes later when Jake received an alert from Lassie that she'd finished the task he'd assigned her. They walked through the office and stepped up to the Glass.

'What do you have for me, Lassie?' asked Jake.

'Have a look at the screen, Jake,' said Lassie.

Jake did as he was told and noted that there were about a dozen possible targets. Five of them were of great interest. 'David, we should notify all of them about this threat. What do you think?'

'That'll be tricky trying to tell them that they are the possible targets of someone we're not even sure has a political focus. Let alone someone we can't even identify,' said David.

'That's true, but we can't sit back and do nothing. It worked when we alerted the PSU. They listened.'

'We'll need to convince Peter that it will be worth alerting these people.'

'Then let's go and speak to him,' said Jake.

'We can't yet, he has someone else with him.'

'Who?'

'Dawn Forde,' said David.

'I reckon she's one of the people, along with Peter, who can help us get this message out.'

'I don't know Peter that well; but he does give me the impression that he doesn't like to be disturbed when he's in a meeting.'

'We can kill two birds with one stone, so to speak,' said Jake. 'I'm going to try.'

'Good luck.'

Jake transferred the current data to his tablet and crossed the floor to Peter's office. He drew a deep breath and knocked on the door.

'Enter!'

Jake opened the door and confidently walked in. 'Excuse me for interrupting, Sir. Good morning, Dawn.'

'This had better be good, North,' replied Peter.

'Sir, sorry to interrupt but I heard that you were with Dawn and I felt I should bring both of you my current discovery.'

Peter glared at him, and Jake became a little nervous.

'When you were at Williams, I heard you would do this sometimes to your CO. I read reports. Very well, show us what you have.'

Jake walked over to the desk, placed his tablet down in front of Peter, invited Dawn to look on and opened the file.

'As you can see, I asked Lassie to predict the possible path from the last event to the centre of town on a spiral arc.'

'We already know this,' said Peter.

'Yes, but I then asked Lassie to isolate some specific target points, following a thought I had.'

'If this isn't relevant, North ...'

'I understand, Sir, but I believe it is very relevant.' Jake took a breath and continued. 'As you can see, the path takes us from the former PSU office in Parkville, down to Kew, through Hawthorn and skirting Richmond.'

'Get to the point, North, I know what's where in Melbourne.'

'Sorry, Sir. I asked Lassie to isolate premises that had any sort of political link. The search returned those now highlighted on the screen. Of most significance are the offices of Vienata Grond-Fiala, leader of the new opposition party.'

'What you're saying is that you believe that she may be the next target?' asked Dawn.

'It's a presumption, Dawn,' said Jake.

'How did you come to this conclusion, North?' said Peter.

'Well, Sir, as I highlighted to you earlier today, Independence Day is the target day, provided our interpretation of the countdown is correct. Then with the attack on the former PSU building, again, I concluded that the ultimate target is political. If this is true, it can stand to reason that the only event left between the PSU attack and Independence Day would be a political target.'

'I must thank you for that information too, corporal,' said Dawn. 'We managed to get everyone out the day before the attack took place. It wasn't easy to covertly move an entire office building in only a few days. Thankfully, our more permanent offices were ready enough for us to move in to. We're still unpacking and several floors are still off limits, but we're managing.'

'Do you think the leader of the opposition is now the next target?' asked Peter.

'Yes I do, Sir. To be safe, we should alert all the politically linked premises in the area of a possible threat next Wednesday,' said Jake.

'Peter, I'd like to pursue this for a moment,' said Dawn. 'If what the corporal is saying is correct, we need to act and act urgently.'

'Thank you, corporal,' said Dawn when Jake had finished his presentation. 'You have been very thorough indeed. Have you had a chance to follow-up the building in the laneway where SSgt Barrow disappeared?'

'Not yet, but I intend to investigate it more thoroughly,' said Jake. 'I've had a couple of preliminary visits. I'm waiting for a specific piece of electronic equipment to arrive. It was supposed to be here last week, but the overseas supplier has had some shipping delays. It should be here soon.'

Jake left Peter's office and walked back to the Glass Room. There he slumped into the nearest chair, somewhat relieved.

'You're one lucky soldier, Jake' said David. 'I'm impressed.'

'I was a nervous wreck before I knocked on the door.'

'You'll find out soon enough how you went. I can see Dawn saying good-bye to Peter.'

'North!'

Jake was startled when he heard his name. He stood and watched as Dawn walked to the lift. He walked into Peter's office, closing the door behind him. He didn't sit, but stood at relaxed attention, looking directly ahead of him out the window.

'Crpl Jake North.'

'Yes, Sir.'

'You have balls for interrupting a meeting when you know damn well you're not supposed to.'

'My apologies, Sir.'

'This time, no apologies are required. I'm very impressed actually. Officers have cringed when I've dressed down people for lesser things, yet you didn't fear that.'

'What I presented I felt was important, so I took the chance to address both of you at once.'

'I want you to prepare me a list of contact names and numbers for those premises you feel are potential targets. I will contact each of them myself. If we can avoid another disaster, then we are doing well. The more we put this person off-guard, the more likely he is to make a mistake.'

'Yes, Sir. I will email you the list right after lunch.'

'Dismissed!'

'Thank you, Sir.' Jake left Peter's office and returned to his desk.

David approached. 'Well I'll be, you're still alive.'

'Only just,' said Jake. 'He wants a list of names and numbers of the potential targets. He's going to contact them himself.'

'You'd better get on with it then.'

'I told him I'd email it after lunch.'

'You cheeky devil. Lunch is on you then.'

'I have no problem with that, David.'

9.2

Jake wandered into work from the underground car park looking despondent. He didn't even see Gabby as she bounded in through the main door.

'Jakey, what's the matter, baby?'

'Oh, Gabby, I didn't see you there,' said Jake, stopping short from bowling her over.

'Oh dear, this looks serious. You'd better come with me.' She grabbed his hand, dragged him to her lab, and sat him down on a stool. 'Tea or coffee?'

Jake looked at her with a small amount of disdain.

'Oh yeah, tea, herbal too.' Gabby faked a disgusted shudder. 'Well, you're in luck Mr Jake, I happen to have a supply of just the right stuff. Now don't move.' She tossed her bag on her desk and went into the small kitchenette she had to one side. Whistling merrily, she went about brewing him a drink. 'One large mug. Check. Herbal tea, fruity too. Very colourful, nice and gay. Check. Vodka. Check.'

Jake looked up suddenly and tried to peer around the corner. (He knew better than to get off the chair Gabby had put him on.)

Gabby came back to where Jake was and saw him looking wide-eyed. 'Now, what's the matter?'

Jake looked away quickly.

'Come on, tell aunty Gabby what's wrong,' she added, pulling up a stool beside him. The kettle began to whistle. 'Hold that thought, I'll be right back.' She dashed away, made

Jake's drink and brought it back. Taking it in his hands, he sat there and looked at it. 'Aren't you going to drink it?'

Jake looked at her and smiled.

'Ohhhh, the vodka thing.' Gabby chuckled. 'I only said that to tease you. I used bourbon instead, now drink.'

Jake hesitated.

'Dri-nk.'

Jake took a sip, let his shoulders fall and smiled.

'Gotcha,' laughed Gabby.

'I never know when you're joking,' said Jake.

'Well, that makes two of us. The times you've caught me out. Let's just say, I have a lot of catching up to do. Now, what's wrong?'

'I was supposed to go away with Anhton this weekend, but his leave was cancelled on Friday morning, so we couldn't go.'

'Bugger. There's more, I can sense it.'

'Then there's the next event that's due to take place this Wednesday. Senator Grond-Fiala refuses to accept that there is a threat. Even when presented with the fact that five of her former army unit buddies are missing, presumed dead.'

'Have you spoken to ...? Who is in charge now, I can't keep up?'

Jake looked at Gabby. 'Oh, it's Cmdr Peter Dugald, from Williams Base.'

'Yes, of course you have,' said Gabby. 'You know he's the President-elect's husband?'

'Yeah, even the president-elect has tried speaking to the senator, as a friend, that she should heed the alert and relocate to a more secure premises. However, she refuses to budge and is treating it as a political stunt to put her off guard,' said Jake.

'What is it with pollies. Why can't they simply believe people when such threats are possible.' She took a sip from her own drink. 'Hey, why haven't you caught this creep?'

'Why haven't you found any prints?' replied Jake.

'Ouch. Fair enough. I've tried every trick in the book. I even heard of a new technique, got the gear and tried that, still nothing. Whoever is doing this, has been really careful when handling these items.'

'He sure has been.'

They sat in silence for a while.

'So, what are you going to do Wednesday night?'

'I'm going to wait at the Senator's offices and try to catch this guy.'

'Will Dugald let you do it?' said Gabby.

'Probably not, so I'm only going to tell David. Then I will deal with what the boss throws at me the next day.'

'I wish you well. You can have your farewell drinks at my place.'

'Thanks for the vote of confidence, Gabby,' said Jake.

'Anytime, my love. You should probably get upstairs and get on with solving this case.'

'Thanks for the cuppa and chat.'

'You're always welcome down here, Jake, you know that.'

Jake put his mug on the bench, gave Gabby a hug, collected his satchel and went to his desk.

Jake entered his area, dropped his satchel and proceeded towards the Glass.

'Crpl North, my office,' called Peter.

Jake winced slightly, changed his direction, and went to Peter's office.

'You're beginning to make a habit of being in my office lately. I hope this isn't the start of a trend?'

'I guess that depends on why I'm here.'

'Yes, true.'

'Why am I here?' asked Jake.

'You're late!'

'I was down with Gabby. She made me a cuppa to cheer me up. It wasn't a good weekend for me.'

'There's something you need to know,' said Peter. 'I've just finished another phone call with the senator and she still refuses to budge.'

'I see. Is there anything else we can do?'

'Yes. I want you to go to her offices and watch for anything unusual.'

'I'll do my best, sir.'

'Well, you seem excited about this job.' He looked him over and watched his eyes and his smile. 'You were already planning to go and do this without telling me, weren't you?'

Jake looked surprised for a moment. 'Yes, I was, sir. I didn't think you'd let me and I was going to tell David just as I left work on Wednesday night. I was prepared to deal with whatever you dished out afterwards.'

'I like your style even more, North. Initiative, balls and a preparedness to face me no matter what.'

'I guess so, sir.'

'Don't guess, North. Do. That's what I liked about you over at Williams. You got your jobs done. I know it made the others look like idiots and I know they disliked you, but I had to be fair and listen to all sides. Secretly, I loved what you did. I may come across as hard-arsed and tyrannical, in a way I am, but it gets the job done. Some of those over at Williams need to move on. Maybe I should put them in with you on a job or two and see how they survive.'

'Thank you, sir,' said Jake. 'Do you think we should notify the senator of our plans?'

'No, I think we can handle this quietly ourselves. Park a distance away, find a spot to be inconspicuous and wait. Make sure David is aware that you have my permission to do this and have all services on standby.'

'Yes, sir. Should we notify the police?'

'I'll deal with the police,' said Peter.

9·3

'Art, I know we didn't win, but I'm sure as hell not going to let things just sit down and die,' said the female across the conference table.

'Calm down, Vienata,' replied Senator Art Donyer, deputy leader of the minor political party in the new republic. 'I wasn't implying that we would. All I was saying was that it won't be easy.'

Senator Vienata Grond-Fiala, let out a huge sigh. Whilst proud of her Italian heritage, she liked to colour her hair. At the moment it was a rich purple. This happened to go well with her hazel eyes and light olive complexion. Since leaving the army after returning with the rest of her unit, Vienata went into politics. As a result, she has allowed some of the perks to get the better of her. She wasn't overweight by any means, but the lithe frame she carried in the army was no longer easily visible.

'Perhaps we should call it a night, Vie?' said Art.

Senator Art Donyer was the opposite to Vienata. Balding, grey eyes, and overweight. His double chin hung heavily beneath his ruddy and puffy face. He was tall, which made him look more like an ogre than a senator. He had been involved with politics for over thirty years and at sixty-five it was showing.

'As head of the Opposition, I need to get these policies finalised.'

'They already are. We've been working on them for almost a year now. They're as ready as they'll ever be.'

'I have to make sure I know them inside out, and so do you. As my deputy leader, you and I are the ones the media will hammer when we seem to change direction or viewpoint. Being a new political environment, we need to cement the views of the party quickly and firmly. How many clichés could I use here to describe the potential damage. *Caught with our pants down? Foot in mouth disease?*'

Art chuckled. Soon Vienata was laughing as well.

'You're right, we should call it a night.' She looked down at her watch. 'Shit, its after midnight. My husband will think I don't exist anymore.'

'As the husband of the leader of the new opposition party, he has to get used to it.' Art rose and stretched. 'Before I lock my office, I'm gonna take a whizz. Be right back.'

'TMI, Art, TMI,' said Vienata, holding up her hand to deflect the comment.

Art waved back at her as he walked down the hall to the bathrooms. As Vienata stepped around her desk, she paused to look at a ceremonial staff that hung on the wall. She stepped forward to look at it more closely.

'I wonder if I can still hold the respect of those that gave this to me,' she said aloud.

Vienata ran her fingers over the intricate designs on the stem. At each end, carved handles allowed the user to hold it before them and wield it as required. They could just as easily hold either end allowing the staff to be used akin to a sword. Picking the staff up, she moved to a part of the office affording her a better area to move about. Going through a series of well-practiced steps, she stretched, lunged, turned and parried. Momentarily, she was lost in the world of her martial arts training whilst in the Army.

She stopped suddenly. Something registered in the corner of her eye. She began to peer through her office window. She walked over to the door. 'Is someone there? Hello? Art?' She looked around the open office area but could see nothing. Returning to her desk, she put the staff down and hurriedly packed her satchel and grabbed her handbag.

Pausing slightly, she had an uneasy sensation that someone was approaching her from behind. She stood and with a glance to her left, she could see the reflection in a window of a darkened figure approaching through her outer office. Picking up the staff, she turned quickly and deftly defended herself as the figure rapidly approached.

Caught off guard, the figure faltered backwards as Vienata skilfully wielded the staff. The dark figure continued to retreat, fending the blows as best it could. Feeling she had an advantage, she began to yell for Art's help. In her moment of slight distraction, the figure thrust an office chair in her direction, which she dodged safely. This allowed the figure the chance to grab a broom handle, remove the broom head and prepare a staff of its own.

Seeing they were equally armed, Vienata stood her ground. The dark figure moved in her direction and she readied herself for the next blow. Staying on her feet, she still found it difficult to defend, but defend she did. As the tribal staff was made of hardwood, the figure's softer broom handle broke in two on contact, such was the force of the thrust. Seizing her opportunity when she saw the indecision in the figure's step, she let fly with a thrust of her own which landed an almighty crack across the figure's left leg, causing it to crumble to the ground.

Vienata began to advance on her attacker. The figure avoided her blows and was able to stand using a desk to put relative safe distance between them. Vienata took a moment to gather breath, and then with two hands firmly on the staff, she began to swing it towards the figure. However, she was met with resistance and when she realised what was happening, the figure had used the momentum of the swinging staff to get himself clear of the desk.

Vienata stopped. There was only one person who knew how to do that, and she had taught him how to do it. She dropped her guard and looked intently at the figure rapidly approaching her. 'Why are you doing this, ...' Her question could not be finished as the figure slammed into her, forcing her backwards onto the corner of a desk, breaking her back.

As she lay in pain, the figure stood over her. She looked into his eyes. The last thing she saw were his hands clasping the sides of her head. She felt nothing more as her head was snapped to the left, killing her instantly.

Slumping to the ground beside the lifeless body of Vienata, the figure massaged his painfully aching left leg. A few minutes later, he was up and moving again. He hobbled along the hall, down the back stairwell, and exited the building the way he came in.

As the figure limped slowly along darkened laneways and semi-darkened street to his small matte-black ute, he wasn't prepared for what sprang from behind a parked car.

'Good evening. We meet again.'

9.4

The figure froze and looked up. In the dim streetlights, Jake saw the coldness of the figure's eyes glare at him.

'In a bit of pain, are we?' said Jake, moving towards the figure and onto the footpath to stop him going anywhere.

The figure grunted.

'I'll take that as a yes.'

Fully alert, Jake was prepared for the charge. Using the figure's own weight, Jake quickly flipped him over his shoulder, the figure landing heavily on its injured leg. Jake wasn't prepared for the rapidity with which the figure jumped up though and wasn't ready when the figure charged. Jake ducked but not quickly enough to prevent the knife wound now searing into his left arm.

Jake dropped his gun, clutched his arm and stared back at the figure. Bleeding and in pain, Jake reached for his gun, but the figure was on him once more. They were locked in a fight with Jake holding the knife away from him until he found the strength to crack the figure's hand on a nearby brick wall. The knife clattered onto the ground and the battle continued. Jake managed to land an elbow onto the figure's injured leg. A cry of pain was released and Jake escaped the grip. Jake scrambled along the ground for his gun and just as he reached it, the figure pounced on his back and landed its own punch onto Jake's deep wound. In sheer agony and fury, Jake bucked like a bronco, knocking the figure off his back and into the nearby garden wall.

The figure began to crawl over the top of Jake again, but Jake swung his legs around and twisted the figure in another direction, causing it to land heavily against a car.

By now, Jake's breath was beginning to become shallow with the blood loss and pain. Jake got to his gun, stood and quickly turned on the figure. As he did, Jake heard his name being called and instinctively turned. The figure, in obvious pain itself, landed one final blow on Jake's chest sending him flying backwards onto the ground. Jake raised his head to see the figure limping heavily around the corner.

Jake lay back on the ground and waited. He saw flashlights reflecting off the sides of the cars and soon they shone directly in his face. Covering his eyes, he swatted at the beams as if they were mosquitos annoying him.

'Lay still,' said a medic, as she began to wrap a bandage around the wound on his arm.

Jake winced and let out a small yelp when the medic finished the bandage.

'Suck on this, sir, it will help with the pain,' said another medic, placing a whistle-like object in his mouth.

'Can you tell me your name?' asked the first medic.

Removing the whistle with his good arm, he replied. 'Cpl Jake North, Defence Force Investigative Service.'

'Sir, you need to keep this in your mouth,' insisted the second, and took the whistle from Jake and put it back in his mouth.

Jake looked from one medic to another, slightly bewildered.

'I have to stop finding you like this, my young friend,' said David.

'Forget about me,' said Jake, removing the whistle once more. 'He went around that corner and was limping. He can't have gotten far. Just get him,' he added, pointing out the direction. Jake quickly put the whistle back in his mouth when he saw the second medic move to do it.

'Don't move,' said David.

'Like I'm about to,' yelled Jake, quickly removing and replacing the whistle, as he watched David disappear around the corner.

9.5

The dark figure limped to his matte-black ute and dropped into the driver's seat. In pain, the figure started the engine and pulled the ute away from the curb. As he did, the rear window shattered, showering him with glass. The man ducked automatically, sideswiped a parked car and then planted the pedal and screeched away. Another gunshot destroyed the left side mirror.

Pulling into a side street, the man reached for the glove compartment, and retrieved a small medical kit. A syringe was taken out and cleared of any air bubbles. Through gritted teeth, he jammed it into his injured leg and within a matter of moments, the drug began to take effect, relieving the immediate pain. As he allowed the drugs to take effect, he reached for his phone. Activating the screen, he tapped a couple of icons until it pulled up tracking software.

'Shit!'

The ute sped its way through the inner north suburbs of Melbourne. The man checked the phone again as he raced through red lights. He darted around one corner to head north along by the museum. Glancing at the phone, he suddenly veered the ute into the path of an oncoming mid-sized SUV. The SUV swerved to miss the ute but was clipped anyway. In the rear-view mirror, the figure watched it spin and slide along the road until it slammed into the barriers of a tram stop. He pulled over and watched people rush to the other car and then towards his. He sped away, almost hitting other pedestrians and cars.

Eventually the figure turned the ute west and headed for the inner western suburbs. He continued to race through red lights and was soon driving into the sub-basement of a warehouse in Williamstown. The figure parked the ute, fell out of the driver's seat and collapsed onto a small cot along one wall. After resting there for an hour, he got up, injected his leg once again and inspected the ute, slamming the side of it with a hand.

He then walked over to a wall, took a marker from its holder and crossed off another face on the board he had.

In the far left corner, a door opened and closed.

9.6

David trotted back to where Jake lay. He could see that paramedics were now taking care of him. He found Dustin, Gabby and Amy standing in the background.

'The police want to talk to you,' said Gabby.

'Thanks, do you know where they are?' asked David.

'Waiting for you at the rear of the building.'

'Thanks, Gabby. You'd better get your kits ready, I reckon you'll need them. I'll meet you out the back as soon as I can.'

'Okay, David. See you soon.'

David walked away and was soon approaching a plain-clothed man standing near the rear door of the senator's offices. David smiled when the man turned.

'Anhton, fancy meeting you here,' said David. 'When are you coming back to DFIS?'

'I never left you,' said Anhton. 'I'm on secondment whilst being on probation at the DFIS. Besides I've always called you when I was at a spiral event.'

'This is true, and here we are again.'

'I wish it were under better circumstances. Follow me, you need to have a look at this.'

'You need to know that Jake was injured tonight,' said David.

Anhton turned, shocked. 'He didn't say he was going to

be out here tonight.'

'He wasn't allowed to say anything to anyone.'

'How is he? I need to go to him,' said Anhton, becoming very worried.

'He will be fine and I will make sure you know which hospital he is taken to, but right now, you have a job to do.'

'David, I have to make sure he's okay. I have to be there for him.'

'He'd be the first to tell you to get back to your job,' said David.

Anhton hung his head. 'Yes he would. This way.'

'If we make this quick, I will see that you are released from duty as soon as possible.'

'Thank you,' said Anhton.

Anhton led David to the third floor and they stepped from the stair well into a corridor.

'The first body is in the men's toilets,' said Anhton, holding open the door.

David walked in to see a body lying in a crumpled heap on the floor. He stepped back into the hallway.

'Who's this one?' asked David.

'Sen. Art Donyer, Sen. Grond-Fiala's deputy' said Anhton. 'The other body is along here.' Anhton led David along the corridor and into an open office area.

David swept his eyes around the room to see the layout and the results of a fight. David turned to see Anhton lifting a sheet from an inert body.

'Sen. Vienata Grond-Fiala,' said Anhton.

'Why won't people listen to us,' said David. He held a finger to his left ear. 'Dustin, Gabby, Amy, bring your kits to the third floor. Dustin and Amy, can I get you to work on the body of Sen. Art Donyer? He's in the men's toilets near the stair well exit. Gabby, please bring my kit with you, we'll work on the body of Sen. Grond-Fiala.'

'We'll be right there,' replied Dustin.

'Thanks guys,' said David. 'Forager 1, do you have a status on our injured warrior?'

'Yes, sir. He's been taken to Melbourne General. The ambulance has just left.'

'Thank you, Forager 1.' David turned to Anhton. 'Go, and drive carefully.'

'Thank you, David. Will you speak to my boss when you see him?' asked Anhton.

'It'll be okay. Go and take care of Jake for us.'

Anhton raced along the corridor and disappeared down the back stairs.

David turned back to begin to look over the body of the dead senator. Gabby arrived moments later. 'Gabby, we need to get this area labelled and photographed before the body is moved.'

'Right.' She unpacked her kit and began to process the scene. As she did so, she began to make mental notes of where everything was. She also took as many photographs as she could to try to help get this problem resolved.

After an hour, David, Dustin, Gabby and Amy had finished their work. David sent the others back to DFIS HQ to begin work on the evidence collected.

'What are you going to do?' Gabby asked.

'I'm going to visit Jake.' David replied. 'I'll meet you back at the lab as soon as I can.'

Just after sunrise, David drove into the parking garage of DFIS HQ. He went directly to Peter's office, knowing he'd be there early that day, waiting for the reports from the night before.

'What happened, David? I hear Jake's in hospital.'

'Yes he is, Peter, but he'll be fine,' said David. 'He'll be allowed home tomorrow and has been told to stay away from work for two weeks.'

'Bugger. Do you think he will stay away though?'

'No,' said David simply.

'Next Monday then?'

'More than likely.'

'Tell me what happened.' Peter indicated for David to have a seat.

For the next two hours, David told Peter all that had happened, except for the exact details of the exchange between Jake and the perpetrator. During the conversation, Gabby interrupted them.

Peter waved her into the office. 'What do you have for us?'

'Not much, sir,' said Gabby. 'I've gone over everything. Twice, to be sure. The only prints we found belonged to the two dead senators. At this stage. There were other prints, old ones. I daresay they will belong to staffers, but we're still checking.'

'I simply cannot believe that someone perpetrating these crimes can leave no evidence behind,' said Peter. 'I've now lost another friend. Danika has lost a worthy opponent. Knowing Vienata, she would not have gone down without a fight.'

'Oh, there was a fight,' said Gabby. 'The furniture was definitely moved about. There was a staff near to the senator's body but only her prints appear on it. I'd say she was using it to defend herself. I also found a broken broom stick on the ground. I'm going to presume this was used by her attacker.'

'Anything on that broken broom stick?' asked David.

'I'm looking again,' said Gabby. 'I need to get back to the lab.'

'Thank you, Gabby,' said Peter. Peter rose and closed the door behind Gabby. 'Where does this leave us, David?'

'I'm going to load all that I know into Lassie and see if she can help.'

'That's a start. Keep me posted.'

'I will, sir.'

David left Peter's office and walked to the Glass room. He entered all the new data into the case file. He had Lassie compile it and when she'd completed that task, David sat back and tried to forecast what might happen next.

'Jake is so much better as this tech stuff than me,' said David aloud.

'What is it you want to know, David,' said Lassie.

'How does he do it, Lassie?'

'Do what, David?'

'Figure it all out. It seemed to come so easily to him,' said David.

'With all due respect, David, he is younger than you. He's also a different person, with different ways of approaching things.'

'I guess so.'

'Besides, David, I only do what you tell me to do. I'm not an independent thinker.'

'Well, what do you call this?'

'Call what?' asked Lassie.

'The way you're talking to me now?'

'I am programmed to deduce a possible course of action by reading body language, recognising various vocal tones and analysing the way a question is asked or posed. If I am correct, the conversation carries along as if it is quite normal. If I am incorrect, the person I am talking with will either say something, or change the way they respond to me. At that point, I stop the process.'

'Oddly enough, I feel better, thanks, Lassie,' said David.

'You are welcome, David. Have you downloaded all the new data into your tablet yet?'

'No, should I?'

'Jake used to always download the latest data after new information had been uploaded and compiled. Then when he came in the next time, he would have more data to upload and compile, and so the process went on. He always has the latest information to review,' said Lassie.

'Then let's do it, Lassie. Let me get my tablet first.' David returned a few minutes later, tablet in hand. 'Talk me though the process, Lassie. I never really took that information in when you were first activated.'

'It will be my pleasure, David.'

Lassie walked David through the whole process, which took no less than fifteen minutes.

'That's all I have to do?' asked David.

'That is correct. Now that you are linked, you only have to press the update button. I check what you have against what I have and update anything that's different, both ways.'

'Will Jake be able to get this data if he isn't in the building?' asked David.

'If he has an active internet connection, he will be able to get the latest information.'

'I'll go and see how he's doing and see what he wants to do. Thank you again, Lassie.'

David grabbed his bag and left the office.

9.7

'Mum, are you alright?' called the young teenage boy, rushing into the hospital room.

'Yes, I am Benny. I'm just so glad to see you two. Come here, Archie,' said Dawn.

Benny and Archie hugged their mother warmly.

'What happened, mum?' asked Benny, as he perched himself on the side of the bed.

'Who brought you down here? Where's Jeremy?'

'Gran did and Jeremy said he had to go away for a few days.'

An older woman walked into the room.

'Mum, thanks for bringing the boys in,' said Dawn.

'When they rang me this morning, I had to,' said Dawn's mum.

Dawn hugged Benny again.

'So, what happened?' asked Benny again, a little wide-eyed. 'The police came to our door and everything this morning.'

'Well, I was finishing late, as you know, and I was driving home. I heard some screeching and looked around to see a dark ute come screaming around the corner ahead of me,' said Dawn.

'Then what happened?' asked Benny.

Dawn looked at Benny. 'I tried to get out of the way, he hit me and spun me around and I ran sideways into the tram barrier.'

'Will you be okay?' asked Archie, his face pale.

'I'll be fine. Thankfully, it was the passenger side that hit the barrier and not my side. I was thrown about but I only have lots of bruises and a few cuts from the glass.'

'Wow,' said Benny quietly.

'I have some more news for you boys as well,' said Dawn, smiling broadly. 'I'm going to have another baby, actually two.'

Dawn's mum gasped and the boys broke into huge smiles. Benny patted his mum's stomach gently.

'Thankfully, the babies are okay, well shaken, but the nurses seem to think that there is no damage,' added Dawn.

'How many weeks, Dawn?' asked her mother.

'They think ten weeks or so, mum. The accident last night happened at the wrong time for the babies, but as I said, the nurses seem to think that everything will be okay. They're going to run some more tests later today. I should be able to come home over the weekend. The bruises will be painful for a few days, so I'm going to need you to help me even more around the home, boys.'

'I'll do what I can for you, mum,' said Benny.

'Thanks, darling,' said Dawn. 'Arch?'

'Yeah, I'll help.'

'I'll come and stay for a week or so as well, Dawn.'

'Thanks, mum, that'd be great.'

'Have you told Jeremy yet, mum?' asked Benny.

'I only found out myself today. I'll give him a call when I get home. You said yourself, he's gone away for a few days.'

* * * * *

Dawn was resting on the couch when she heard the front door open.

'Yoo-hoo,' called the voice.

'Jeremy, I'm in the lounge room, sweetie,' said Dawn.

Jeremy limped into the room to see Dawn lying down. 'What's the matter?'

'I was involved in a hit-and-run on Wednesday night. A black ute came out of nowhere. I have no idea what happened to the ute, but my car was written off. I only came out of hospital today. I was going to ring you tonight.'

Jeremy hugged Dawn, who winced slightly.

'Ow.'

'Sorry,' said Jeremy.

'It's okay.'

'Oh my god, Dawn, you should've tried to call me. I would've come home right away.'

'What happened to you?' asked Dawn.

'I had a bit of a fall while I was away. Nothing serious. Some bad bruising, I'll be fine in a few weeks,' said Jeremy.

'We've both been in the wars. Sit, I have more news for you.'

Jeremy sat on the end of the couch, lifted Dawn's legs onto his and began to gently massage them.

'Don't worry about another car, I have a spare Forden I'll give you. I'll bring it over tomorrow. Just remember to get it on the register for Wednesday though.'

'You don't have to do that,' said Dawn.

'Yes I do.'

Dawn laid her head back on the cushions. 'That feels so nice. I've missed that.'

'So, what's this news?'

'I'm pregnant.'

Jeremy stopped massaging and looked at Dawn. 'You're what? That's fantastic.' He reached over and gently pressed his hand against her stomach. 'Do the boys know?'

'Yeah, I told them when they visited me Thursday in hospital. Thankfully, the babies are okay. I still have to go to my own doctor to get a referral and have them checked by a gynaecologist.'

'Did you say babies?'

'Yeah, we're having twins.'

'Oh my god,' said Jeremy.

'I'll give you a call when I know about any appointment so you can come as well.'

'Okay.'

9.8

Anhton had brought Jake home from the hospital and he was now sitting in his courtyard, soaking up the warm November sun. Anhton was getting dinner ready when the doorbell rang.

'I'll get it,' said Jake. 'I need to keep moving.'

'You need to rest, hon. I can get that.'

Jake ignored Anhton and walked through the kitchen to let David in.

'Glad to see you up and about, Jake.'

'Good to see you too, David. If you've come to check, I've been looking over all the data from last Wednesday night. I'm up-to-date and will be in the office tomorrow.'

'We wish you'd stay at home, like the doctor has instructed,' said David.

'You know I can't. Independence Day is this Wednesday and I have to work out what's going on before then.'

'I had to try.'

Jake smiled and showed David to the courtyard.

'Beer? Cider?' Jake asked.

'A cider would be great.'

Jake went back inside and came out with two ciders. Anhton appeared a few minutes later.

'Hey, David. Good to see you. Cheers.'

They tapped their bottles and took a drink.

'You too, Anhton.'

They sipped their ciders and watched the sun begin to go down.

'Will you stay for dinner, David?' asked Jake.

'I can't, sorry. I was dropping by to make sure you were home, and to make sure I couldn't convince you to stay here for a few more days.'

Jake laughed. 'That's fine. I'll see you at work tomorrow?'

'Yes you will,' said David. 'I'd better get going.'

David rose and Jake followed him to the door.

Jake returned to the kitchen. 'How long before dinner, sweetie?'

'Twenty minutes, I guess,' said Anhton.

'Cool. I'm going to sit and meditate for a while.'

Jake fetched his yoga mat, changed into some comfortable clothing and set himself up in the backyard. With the sun warming his back, he digested all that had happened.

- Two senators killed, one being the leader of the new opposition party,

- Senator Grond-Fiala was also a member of the same army unit as Vic, Linda, Garthen, Damian and Derik,

- That leaves only four of the unit still alive,

- The President-elect is one of those still alive and is the most likely target,

- Must check all political venues for the Independence Day celebrations and official proceedings.

Jake finished just as Anhton was coming out of the house. After Jake had put away his yoga mat, he and Anhton enjoyed their meal together.

10.1

Dawn Forde drove her new Forden to the gate of the parking garage for the Trialto Towers and arrived just before six in the morning. She stopped where the guard indicated and rolled down her window.

'Good morning, Ms Forde,' said the guard.

'Morning, Gavin,' replied Dawn. 'How's it going?'

'All good so far. I see you have a new car, and a Forden. Have you registered it?'

'I only got it Monday night so I registered it yesterday . Mine was involved in an accident and a friend loaned me his for the moment.'

'Is it safe?' asked Gavin.

'I trust the man who gave me this, and no it hasn't been checked. Do what you have to do.' Dawn smiled but was now impatient.

Gavin stepped into the hut and retrieved a mirror on a long pole and began to search underneath the SUV. He moved around it carefully, allowing his time to make sure nothing was untoward.

Dawn leant out her window. 'You going to be long, Gavin? I'm feeling sick and need to get to a bathroom.'

'Just about done, Ms Forde.'

Gavin walked past the front of the car and then stopped at her open window. 'All done. Nothing unusual.'

'Thank you, Gavin. Happy Independence Day.'

'To you as well, Ms Forde.'

Gavin stepped inside the gatehouse and opened the boom gate for her. She drove her Forden AV to the upper level where the Presidential parking was located. She rushed to the bathroom in the lobby but was soon traveling to the 65th floor where President-elect Danika Wordsworth had her offices.

Dawn was surprised to see Danika at her desk.

'Good morning, Madam President,' said Dawn, a smile stretching across her face.

"I'll have to get used to that, won't I?'

'Yes you will.'

Dawn returned the hug that Danika was offering.

'Now, why are you here so early? Did you even go home yesterday?' asked Dawn.

'Yes, I went home, but couldn't sleep. I've only been here about thirty minutes, and I've been going over my inauguration speech. Giulia should be here soon.'

'Right, I'll go over the last few details and make sure this day is the best day in our history.'

Dawn left the President's office and returned to her own.

10.2

Anhton walked bleary eyed into the kitchen to see Jake preparing a large breakfast.

'Sorry I was so restless last night, sweetie,' said Jake.

A strange electronic device beeped on the bench.

'At least you went and slept in the other bed, if you didn't I was going to. What's the matter?' said Anhton.

'I just couldn't stop thinking about today and what might happen. I need to get to that warehouse in William-stown today, it's been bugging me for so long now and finally my new equipment arrived yesterday.'

The machine beeped again.

'What is that thing?' asked Anhton. 'I saw it yesterday. It looked like a nasty jigsaw puzzle to me,' added Anhton indicating the array of electronic components spread on the bench.

'It's a device that will hopefully allow me to find any hidden entrances that are electronically operated.'

'You think there's an entrance, other than the roller door at the back, that allows someone to come and go?'

'Yes I do. That's the only way Linda could've vanished,' said Jake. 'I didn't hear any roller door open and close that night and if it had, there would've been time for me to get inside. There has to be another way. You're coming with me.'

'Am I now?'

'Yes you are. I'll need your muscles. I'm still so weak

after last week.'

'Yeah, right. You weren't that weak last night,' said Anhton.

Jake blushed a little.

'Okay, I'd very much like you to come along with me today.'

'I'd love to. You might need my muscles to help you.'

Jake rolled his eyes and laughed. 'Here, have some brekky.'

When they'd finished, they jumped into Jake's car and went to the DFIS offices. They went to Jake's desk gathered his field kit and made sure there was no more information that had come in overnight.

'Morning, Jake. Anhton.'

Jake turned to see Peter in a suit and not his regulation Defence Force Dress uniform.

'Sir?'

'Today I become the First Husband of Basslea,' said Peter. 'As such, I officially retired from the Defence Force as of yesterday.' 'I knew you were the Madam President's husband, but I thought you'd be at least able to stay with Defence,' he said.

'We tried, but the boffins who drew up the new constitution didn't feel it was right. It'd be the same for a spouse of a male president. They'd have to give up whatever they did to be by his side.'

'I understand,' said Jake.

'What are you up to today?' said Peter. 'Shouldn't you be coming into town?'

'I'll try and get in later, Peter. I really have to get a look at that warehouse in Williamstown. I couldn't sleep last night thinking about it. It has significance to today and I need to find out why.'

'Make sure someone knows where you are and that you have back up,' said Peter.

'I'm taking Anhton with me. I'm sure we'll be fine.'

'Okay then. Well, good luck and I want to be the first to know when you catch whoever it is that's been troubling us all year. Happy Independence Day.'

'Happy Independence Day to you too.'

10.3

By nine o'clock, Dawn had gone over the plans for the hundredth time and had confirmation from her staff that everything was in place. The Presidential procession was meant to go from the Trialto Towers to Government House and then to the Parliament buildings afterwards. She sat back in her chair and turned to look out the window. The day had dawned clear and fresh. The weather forecast was for a mild, sunny day. Dawn allowed herself a smile. Her phone rang.

Picking up the phone, she focussed on her desk once more. 'Good morning, this is Dawn Forde ... Good morning Dr Forsythe. How can I help you? ... Yes, that's correct ... Oh, I see. Is anything the matter? ... You're sure though? ... Can it wait a few days? I have the President to deliver to Government House this morning ... Very well, I'll call you next week to make the appointment ... Happy Independence Day.' Dawn pressed the button to terminate the call and dialled another number. 'Jeremy, it's Dawn ... Yes, very busy ... I love you too. I just had a call from the paediatric surgeon from the hospital and they want to see me again ... She didn't say there was, but wanted to run a couple more tests ... I want to make sure you'll be available next week? ... Again? You're going away a lot lately ... I know, I know ... Don't forget, we're invited to the official Presidential ball tonight ... Okay, I'll talk to you later.'

Dawn put the phone on its cradle. A knock at her door distracted her.

'Dawn, the President would like to see you,' said Giulia.

'Okay, Giulia, I'll be right there.' Dawn looked around her office, gathered what she needed and followed Giulia to the President's office. When she arrived, she was surprised to see Cmdr Peter Dugald waiting there. She greeted him warmly. 'Good morning, Peter, it's good to see you.

'Likewise, Dawn.'

'What brings you here?'

'Well, I had this strange message delivered to me to say that I was needed at the President's office as part of the official party,' said Peter.

'When did this change, Giulia?' asked Dawn.

'It didn't,' said Giulia.

'Did you ask him to be here, Madam President?'

'No. He was supposed to meet me at Government House though,' said Danika.

'That shouldn't be a problem,' said Dawn. 'Excuse my bluntness, but were you screened correctly as you came in, Peter?'

'Yes I was,' said Peter.

'I can send it down the line that you'll be travelling with the President,' said Dawn. 'We have an hour before we have to start rolling, stay here and relax.'

10.4

A fair-haired, strongly built man in his mid-forties walked up to the check-in counter. The attendant took the ticket and passport from him.

'Good morning, Mr Healey. Welcome to Air Canada,' said the man behind the counter.

'Thank you,' replied Mr Healey. 'I was hoping to have been here earlier, but traffic and last minute business held me up.'

'You have plenty of time to go through passport control. You have two hours before we start boarding.'

'That's good to know,' said Mr Healey.

'Aisle or window seat today?'

'I didn't think it mattered in business.'

'Not really. Once you're in the air, you'll be free to move around. You still need to be booked into a seat,' said the attendant.

'Window, please.'

'All done, Mr Healey, enjoy your flight.'

'Thank you,' said Mr Healey. He walked off towards the gate to passport control.

10.5

Jake sat on the ground going over the instructions for the third time trying to get his new electronic device to work. 'I knew I should've read all this properly last night.'

'Explain to me what this does again?' asked Anhton, as he lay against the wall of the warehouse in Williamstown.

'This device will allow me to detect the presence of, and hopefully unlock, any electronic system used to lock a premises.'

'You think that's what's here?'

'Yes.' The device beeped once, then three more times. 'Ah, got it. It just needed to register. Let's get to work.'

'That only took you thirty minutes. You know the Presidential parade starts in an hour from the Trialto Towers?' said Anhton.

'I know this.'

'I thought you wanted to be there for it.'

'I do,' said Jake.

'Why are we still here then?'

'I have to find out why this building is significant. You know I couldn't sleep last night.'

'Don't remind me.'

'Let's hope this works.' Jake stood and began to move the scanner over the brickwork of the warehouse.

'How long is this going to take?'

'Until it works.'

'How long's a piece of string?' Anhton muttered to himself.

'I heard that!'

Jake turned the corner and moved slowly along the wall. About ten metres from the corner, heading along the alley towards the main street, the device began to light up. Soon all the indicator lights went green.

'This is it. The door is here somewhere,' said Jake.

'Now what?' asked Anhton.

'I switch to unlock mode.' Jake pressed a few buttons on the device and the screen began to flick through combinations of numbers and letters at a very rapid pace. Suddenly, the device stopped scanning and beeped loudly. As it did, the wall began to move. Anhton quickly had his gun out and in front of him. Jake stepped back, drew his gun and activated his torch. They both peered into the inky blackness of the void beyond the door.

Stepping cautiously, Jake moved inside. Anhton, now with his torch activated, followed. The combined beams were strong enough for them see that no one was inside. Once they had cleared the door, it automatically shut behind them, darkening the room significantly. Jake moved his torch around and saw the controls for a lift on the opposite wall. Moving the beam slightly to the right, he saw a switch. Removing his handkerchief from his pocket, he flicked the switch, which activated the light for the entry room. Next, he called for the lift.

While they waited, Jake retrieved a headpiece from his backpack. Placing it on his head, he adjusted it and then proceeded to link it to his phone. He dialled a number.

'David, can you hear me? ... Good ... Are you receiving vision? ... Good ... As you can see, we've found a way inside. The lift has just arrived. I hope you're recording all this? I'll leave the channel open.'

Standing back, Jake and Anhton watched as the lift doors opened, guns at the ready. When they saw that the lift was empty, they checked to see that there were no traps inside. When they felt it was safe, the stepped in and the door closed. The lift automatically went down. The two men were wary and kept their guns ready. When the lift stopped, and the doors opened, they flattened themselves against the sides. The doors opened, but nothing, or no one, entered. Guns before them, torches lighting their way, they stepped into a vast underground room.

'I'll try and find a master light switch, David. Hold on. Keep recording.'

After searching the walls, Jake found what he hoped was the switch. He flicked it and it worked, the overhead lights came on, revealing an array of vehicles and machines.

'This is well organised. I'll see what else I can find,' said Jake.

Jake and Anhton began to carefully move about the items, careful not to touch anything. Jake looked up and down the ramp so that David could catch the vision. Jake then walked slowly around the three vehicles; one a small matte-black ute, the second a slightly larger matte-black utility and the third a matte-black tow truck.

Jake then spotted the green drums, but the smell reached him before he could get too close. Stepping away, he focussed on the press with its pile of heavy disks nearby. Along one wall, he saw a small desk and eating utensils. Nearby, Jake found a camp stretcher and small table with medical supplies.

'Jake, I think you should come and have a look at this,' called Anhton in a serious tone.

Jake carefully picked his way to where Anhton was standing. 'Oh my god.'

10.6

Dawn stood from behind her desk, straightened her clothes, acknowledged the two gentlemen standing at her door and walked down the hall to the President's office. 'Madam President, it's time to go.'

The President turned and nodded her head towards Dawn. Clasping her husband's hand, Danika and Peter walked from the office. Danika's long-time, former fellow army unit soldier and now personal secretary, Giulia, beamed. They followed Dawn towards the lift and waited for it to arrive.

'When we step from the lift, we will be shielded by a temporary wall. That will allow you time to prepare yourself for the media beyond and your destiny beyond that,' said Dawn.

'I understand,' said Danika.

The lift arrived and they all stepped in.

10.7

Passengers waiting to board the flight were fixed on the screens of varying devices. The proceedings happening in the heart of Melbourne transfixed them all. One passenger leant casually against a far wall, trying to be inconspicuous about his viewing.

'Attention passengers, would Mr Austin Healey please make himself known to the staff at the Air Canada gate desk?'

Pushing himself away from the wall, he carefully took his hands from his jacket pocket. Zipping the pocket closed, he went over to the counter.

'I'm Austin Healey, is something the matter?'

'No, Mr Healey, there is nothing wrong, except that when you checked in, the attendant was supposed to let you know that your meals between Melbourne and Honolulu have been mixed and we are unable to supply your dietary requirements.'

Austin sighed imperceptibly. 'That's ok, it's not that critical, and it's only a couple of meals.'

'We have managed to arrange last minute alternatives. Here is the list,' said the attendant.

Austin took the list, nodded and returned it. 'They will be fine.'

'Thank you for your understanding, Mr Healey. When you arrive in Vancouver, speak to our office at the airport and they will reimburse you accordingly.'

Austin simply nodded and re-focussed his attention on the television screen filled with the Independence Day celebrations. He went back to his position against the wall. Slipped his hands back into his pockets, slipped it inside a glove and felt for the small mobile phone he had there.

Just then, the announcement was made for passengers to begin boarding. There was an excitement in the air. People really didn't want to board their plane just yet, they wanted to see what was happening with the proceedings.

The plane loaded quickly and the passengers were treated to the proceedings by being able to watch it on the screens inside the cabin. The only time they went off was for the safety demonstration, but once that had finished, the telecast was broadcast once more.

Austin sat comfortably in his business class seat and unobtrusively, placed his hand in his pocket, pulled it back out with the glove on and the small phone resting in his palm. He began to dial a series of numbers as the plane turned to begin its take-off.

As the engines roared, Austin pressed the send button. As soon as he knew the signal had been received, the phone was switched to flight mode and all data was in the process of being removed. At that moment, the screens were also switched off, much to the annoyance of the rest of the passengers.

10.8

Jake stood next to Anhton and stared in disbelief at the wall.

'David, are you seeing this? I'll put you on speaker, that way we can both talk to you.' Jake pressed an icon on his phone.

'David?'

'I'm here,' said David. 'Look at the wall again, Jake.'

Jake raised his head and moved it slowly over the wall that had nine pictures

'Whilst the pictures show the people in army uniforms, they are all about ten years old, it's unmistakable who they are,' said Jake.

'It's the Army unit,' said David. 'With one face very noticeably missing.'

'Jeremy's. We need to find out where he is and bring him in. We also need to get this place thoroughly dusted. We may need a little help with this one.' Jake turned to indicate the basement area.

'Yeah, I can see that,' said David.

'We have to let the rest of the army unit know.'

'Jake, have a look at this,' called Anhton.

'Hang on, Anhton's found something else.'

Anhton had moved further along the wall from where Jake had been standing showing David the photo wall.

'Shit! Shit, shit, shit, shit!' said Jake, shaking. Jake pulled the headset off so that he could focus the camera on his own face. 'David, look at me. I don't care what you have to do or who you have to call, but you have to evacuate the Trialto Towers.'

'When?' said David.

'What do you mean 'When', David?' said Anhton, poking his head in beside Jake's.

'Immediately, that's when. Like five hours ago, that's when,' said Jake urgently.

'You do realise what's happening right now?' said David.

'Don't argue, just do it,' said Jake.

'Jake?'

'I'm not joking. Have a look at this.' Jake replaced the headset and steadied his head so that David could focus on the map that was pinned to the wall.

A map of the central business district of Melbourne.

A map that had a big 'X' right where the towers were located.

'Can't you see what the target is, David?' said Anhton.

'David?'

David didn't respond.

David couldn't respond.

10.9

'We now change our vision to the waiting cars at the base of the Trialto Towers,' said the TV announcer. 'We believe the President is in the elevator, bringing her down to begin the greatest moment in our history. At eleven o'clock this morning, she will sign the charter that formally declares the Republic of Basslea a reality. It's an exciting time for everyone ...'

BOOM!

10.10

'David, are you still there?' asked Jake.

Silence.

'David, what's going on?'

'It's too late, Jake,' said David

'What do you mean it's too late?'

'What happened?'

Jake threw off his headset and raced outside. He ran down the alley and into the street. He looked around urgently for another street or a way to get higher. He raced in through the front of the building.

'Do you have access to the internet on your computer?' Jake asked the person behind the front desk.

'Yes I do,' said the woman. 'Who are you?'

Jake flashed his credentials. 'I need to see the news of today's events.'

'I'm not allowed to view that here, sorry.'

'If anything happens, refer your boss to me. I need to see what's going on.'

The woman tapped away at the keyboard and accessed one of the news websites. When she saw the vision, she began to weep softly. Jake was transfixed for several minutes.

Eventually he walked away from the desk and outside the building. Anhton was there to greet him.

Jake collapsed into Anhton's arms and cried.

'What happened?' asked Anhton.

'Jeremy blew up the Trialto,' said Jake, wiping away the tears. 'He fucking blew everyone to pieces.'

'Oh shit.' Anhton took hold Jake once more and they hugged.

10.11

Thirty minutes into the flight, when the plane had started to level out at its cruising altitude, the captain made an announcement. 'Good afternoon passengers, it is with much sadness and regret that I must inform you that as we were lifting off this morning, the Trialto Towers in the heart of Melbourne were destroyed by a bomb. We've just had word that all travel has now been suspended to and from Melbourne. We seem to be the last plane allowed to depart. Our hearts and thoughts go out to the many people who lost lives and family members today. I would ask you observe a minute's silence with myself and the crew in honour of the dead.'

If the plane wasn't quiet before, it certainly was now.

'When they are ready, your cabin crew will move through the plane in preparation for lunch,' said the captain. 'Thank you, and we hope you are able to enjoy the flight.'

After the silence, the crew began to prepare the carts. Twenty minutes later, they began to move through the cabin. Ahead of the lunch carts, drinks were served. Austin ordered a cold beer and settled back to listen to his music.